# JUNGLE
# OF BONES

## ALSO BY
### BEN MIKAELSEN:

# JUNGLE OF BONES

## BEN MIKAELSEN

SCHOLASTIC PRESS
NEW YORK

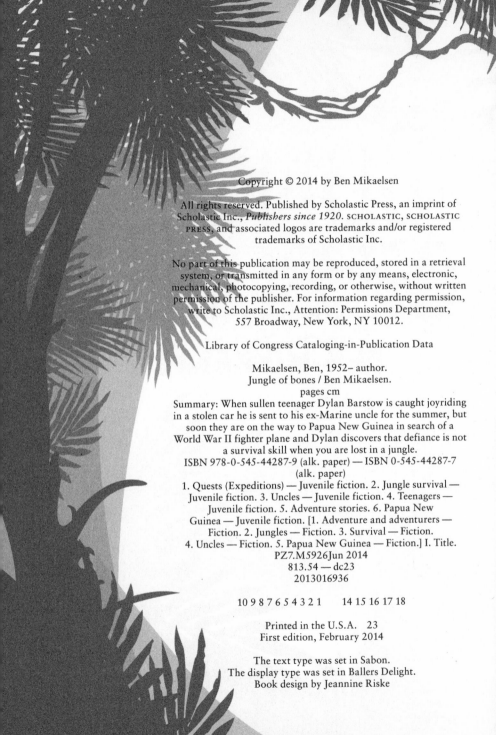

Library of Congress Cataloging-in-Publication Data

Mikaelsen, Ben, 1952– author.
Jungle of bones / Ben Mikaelsen.
pages cm
Summary: When sullen teenager Dylan Barstow is caught joyriding
in a stolen car he is sent to his ex-Marine uncle for the summer, but
soon they are on the way to Papua New Guinea in search of a
World War II fighter plane and Dylan discovers that defiance is not
a survival skill when you are lost in a jungle.
ISBN 978-0-545-44287-9 (alk. paper) — ISBN 0-545-44287-7
(alk. paper)
1. Quests (Expeditions) — Juvenile fiction. 2. Jungle survival —
Juvenile fiction. 3. Uncles — Juvenile fiction. 4. Teenagers —
Juvenile fiction. 5. Adventure stories. 6. Papua New
Guinea — Juvenile fiction. [1. Adventure and adventurers —
Fiction. 2. Jungles — Fiction. 3. Survival — Fiction.
4. Uncles — Fiction. 5. Papua New Guinea — Fiction.] I. Title.
PZ7.M5926Jun 2014
813.54 — dc23
2013016936

10 9 8 7 6 5 4 3 2 1     14 15 16 17 18

Printed in the U.S.A.   23
First edition, February 2014

The text type was set in Sabon.
The display type was set in Ballers Delight.
Book design by Jeannine Riske

I want to dedicate *Jungle of Bones* to the young and courageous crews who manned the bombers during the Second World War. All citizens of our great country need to learn from these brave men that "freedom is never free."

# PROLOGUE

Dylan slogged through the swamp toward the trees. He needed to find dry ground where he could spend the night again. Still he watched for snakes and crocodiles. The air reeked of rotting undergrowth. All day he had seen birds, rats, possums, and other animals to eat, but no way to catch them. The only critters Dylan could approach were snakes and crocodiles. He knew the snakes might be poisonous, and there was no way he was going to try to catch a crocodile, even a small one.

Before leaving the tall grasses, Dylan ate a few more grasshoppers, and then deliberately headed for a root-tangled path entering the jungle. Soon, the thick, matted screen of overhead vines and leaves muted any fading sunlight that made it through the clouds. For the next hour, Dylan stumbled along a trail, no longer looking down to pick his footing. He had to find some kind of refuge before dark, a place where he could be out in the open but on higher ground. He needed a space where he could lie down and still see wild animals approaching. Hopefully a place with fewer insects.

As the light faded, a brief shower of rain fell. Only a few drops penetrated the dense canopy overhead. Suddenly a sharp pain stabbed Dylan's ankle. He glanced down in time to see a dark brown snake recoil and slither across the trail and into the undergrowth. "Ouch," he muttered, crouching. He pulled up his right pant leg to find four small puncture wounds where the snake had sunk its fangs.

Without thinking, Dylan panicked and began running down the trail. But even as he ran, he realized it was probably the dumbest thing he could do after a snake bite. Still he kept running. If he stopped, he would just die here on some muddy overgrown trail in the jungles of Papua New Guinea. By morning, rats would have picked his bones clean. By next week, other critters would have his bones scattered through the forest like twigs and branches. The world would never even know what had happened to Dylan Barstow.

Dylan ran faster. He had to find protection or help.

Overhead the light had faded into darkness. Now the only light came from a hazy moon hanging in the sky like a dim lightbulb. At that very instant, Dylan broke into a clearing similar to the one where he had slept the night before. He walked out away from the darkness of the trees into the moonlight and froze in shock. Ahead were rocks, and next to the rocks stood a tall spiral tree that looked like a big screw. This was the same place he had left early this morning. Without a compass, he had walked all day in a huge circle, only to end up back where he had begun.

Dylan blinked his eyes, as if doing so might make the stupid tree disappear. He shook his head as a wave of despair washed over him, worse than any chill or fever. Dylan screamed, desperate and primal, his voice piercing the hush that had fallen over the clearing. As he finished, tears started down his cheeks, stopping to rest each time he hiccupped with grief. And then a different spasm flooded through his body, and his knees buckled. Dylan collapsed to the ground. The jungle spun in circles. He felt suddenly stiff and cold, as if his body were freezing in a blizzard.

And then there was nothing.

# CHAPTER 1

"Remove your hat, son," the old man said, his voice matter-of-fact, his deep-set eyes intense.

"You're not my dad!" Dylan snapped. "Get out of my face."

The man glared at Dylan, hesitated, then turned back to keep watching the parade.

Dylan's mother, Natalie, turned to him. "Take your hat off," she said quietly.

When Dylan rolled his eyes, she reached out and grabbed his hat, motioning to the old people marching past. "Those men and women are the VFW, the Veterans of Foreign Wars. Remove your hat to show respect."

"Bunch of over-the-hill Boy Scouts with their dumb little hats," Dylan said, motioning. "I can leave my hat on if I want. It's a free country."

Frustration clouded Natalie's eyes as she tucked Dylan's hat into her purse.

"Give that back," Dylan demanded.

She ignored him and headed back toward the car.

"Hey, the parade's not over yet," Dylan said.

Natalie kept walking.

"What's the big deal?" Dylan muttered, following her.

When they arrived home, Dylan's mother worked around the house, giving him the silent treatment. Dylan knew he should feel lucky. Some parents yelled and shouted, or even hit their kids, when they were mad. His mom just clammed up. He could tell whenever she was angry because she quit talking. Dylan stomped up the stairs to his room, whistling for his dog, Zipper, to follow him. His black lab was the only sane thing in his life anymore. Zipper didn't care what anybody wore or said. He didn't care what time anybody went to bed or if they skipped school, as long as he could cuddle and get his ears scratched.

Dylan slammed the door to his room and flopped down on his bed. "C'mon up, boy," he said, coaxing Zipper onto the bed. That was something that bugged his mom; she said Zipper shed too much. But right now Dylan wanted the company. He lay back and stared at the ceiling. It wasn't like he had killed anybody or stolen anything. All he had done was not take his hat off. Since when was that a capital offense? Dylan looked around his room. He was too mad to play his computer games. Instead he took a tennis ball and bounced it repeatedly off the wall. That was something that *really* bugged Mom.

Most times Zipper would chase the ball around the room. Tonight, he curled on the bed, watching with lazy eyes.

"Are you giving me the silent treatment, too?" Dylan asked.

Zipper closed his eyes without even wagging his tail.

Natalie called up, "There's food in the refrigerator if you're hungry. I want you home tonight." Before Dylan could answer, the front door closed. Moments later, the car pulled from the driveway.

Dylan threw the tennis ball extra hard one last time. She hadn't made dinner for him, or said anything about bouncing the ball. What was the big deal not taking his hat off in front of a bunch of old geezers? But deep inside, Dylan knew it was much more than that.

Zipper shifted positions and plopped his nose on Dylan's lap.

Dylan's eyes grew glassy as he scratched behind the dog's ear.

———

It was after dark when Dylan's mother finally returned. He could hear her busying around downstairs for almost an hour. Before going to bed, she poked her head in Dylan's room to make sure he was home.

"What's wrong? Don't you trust me?" Dylan shouted as his mom closed the door. She retreated down the stairs without even saying hello.

Dylan's face flushed with anger. Why did she treat him like some little kid who needed babysitting? He would be in eighth grade this fall, yet she always acted like he was some screw-up who was about to set the house on fire. Dylan crossed the room. If she wanted a screw-up, he would really give her one. He eased his window open and crawled out onto the porch roof. He whispered back, "Zipper, stay!" Dylan could hear Zipper whining as he carefully tiptoed down the shingles and over to where a big maple tree grew near the gutter downspout. With practiced ease, he lowered himself to the ground.

He didn't know where he was going — he just began walking. When he reached the end of the block, an idea struck him. He quickened his pace and ran the next six blocks to the edge of town, where he squeezed under a wood-slatted fence that guarded the front of the local junkyard. Often, when he skipped school, he came out here to wander around the junked cars. He loved cars, any kind of car: antiques, hot rods, sports cars. He especially liked Corvettes — that had been Dad's favorite car. Dylan could tell just about every model that had ever been made. Not that there were any Corvettes in this junkyard, but there were other old cars that were pretty awesome.

Whenever Dylan wandered through this junkyard, the owner, a guy called Mantz Krogan, watched him as if he thought a crook were trying to steal something. To bug the owner, Dylan always walked extra slowly. During one of his visits, Dylan had noticed six or seven cars parked away from the others in a row beside the garage. He asked about them, and Mantz said they had been fixed up to run and were for sale. When Dylan looked inside the cars, he noticed keys in all the ignitions. That was something he remembered now as he crossed the darkened yard.

He walked straight to an old gray Plymouth in the middle of the row. A dim yard light cast eerie shadows from each car. Peering in, Dylan saw a key chain dangling from the car's ignition. He took a step back from the Plymouth and stood up straight. Maybe this wasn't such a good idea. He looked around at the empty and quiet lot. Most people were fast asleep by now, including his mom. If he just took the car for a quick ride and returned it, how would anyone know it was him? Dylan tried the driver's door. He expected it to be locked, but the handle clicked and the door swung open with a creak. Dylan took this as a sign and crawled inside.

Fumbling in the darkness, he stepped on the clutch, shifted it into neutral, and turned the key. The engine cranked several times before the old Plymouth growled to life. Dylan revved the engine. Grinning with nervousness, he slowly shifted the car into reverse and backed away from the building.

A freshly plowed field surrounded the junkyard, looking like a moonscape in the dim light. Dylan floored the gas pedal and popped the clutch, spinning the tires all the way down the gravel drive that circled the yard. When he reached the field, he twisted the steering wheel to the right and heard the twang of wire as the big car plowed through the fence.

Dylan left the lights off — the dim moon made the field look foreboding. Dylan imagined zombies appearing.

This far from the highway, on a dark night, Dylan doubted that anybody would even hear or see him. He shifted into second and floored the gas pedal again. The old Plymouth roared as it bounced across the deep furrows. Again and again the shock absorbers bottomed out, jarring the whole car. Dylan laughed aloud as he spun the wheel and began spinning circles. Dylan called it "cutting donuts."

Careening around in circles made the dry dirt kick up. Soon, a cloud of dust blocked even the half-moon from witnessing his joyride. In total darkness, Dylan kept the gas pedal pressed to the floor. His mom would be having a batch of kittens if she knew that her "little boy" was out spinning donuts in a farmer's field. Dylan closed his eyes and tilted his head back. Keeping the gas pedal floored, he smiled. Life was good!

It was nearly five minutes before Dylan opened his eyes again. He noticed a flicker of red through the thick cloud of dust and let up on the gas pedal. As the dust cleared, the moonlight returned, along with a set of headlights. Without the motor revving, Dylan could also hear a siren now. He straightened out the steering wheel and carefully drove out of the vanishing dust cloud.

Facing Dylan waited two patrol cars, red lights flashing, sirens wailing. "Stop the car and get out with your hands up!" an amplified voice shouted over a loudspeaker on top of one of the squad cars. "Get out *now*!"

Bright headlights blinded Dylan as he braked to a stop and shut off the engine. This was bad. His plan hadn't been to get caught. He panicked. Maybe he could jump out and run — in the darkness the officers probably couldn't catch him. But before Dylan could do anything, a deputy ran to the side of the old Plymouth. He jerked the door open and drew his pistol. "Get out with your hands up!" he shouted.

Dylan turned the ignition switch off and raised his hands. An eerie silence hung in the air, along with dust, as he crawled slowly from the car. "I-I was just having a little fun," he stammered, holding his hands above his head. He recognized the deputy.

"Put your hands on the hood and spread your legs!" the deputy demanded.

Now an officer from the other squad car ran up. He grabbed Dylan's hands, one at a time, and twisted them behind his back to snap on a pair of handcuffs. "You call this a little fun? Wrecking somebody's car, running down a fence, and ripping up somebody's planted field?"

"I'll pay for it," Dylan argued, his voice shaking. The handcuffs bit into his wrists.

"You bet you will," the deputy answered.

Dylan kicked at the dirt in frustration as the officer led him through clouds of dust to the back of the patrol car.

———

At the detention center, Dylan recognized the tall officer who processed him. He also recognized the small room with a big table where he sat across from the officer for questioning. This was where he had come several times before. Last time it had been for stealing candy bars. You would have thought he'd robbed Fort Knox.

The questioning seemed to last for hours. What was so different about this visit? They already had a file as thick as a phone book on him. Tonight the officer treated him like a real criminal, leaving the handcuffs on him and never cracking a smile. He acted as if he was interviewing a serial killer.

He said this was grand theft auto and would be treated as a felony.

Dylan slumped in his chair and tried not to look at the officer. It wasn't like he had really stolen a car. He just took an old junker for a little ride. What was so bad about that?

Finally the officer escorted Dylan to a bare white holding room where he flopped himself onto a thin mattress that covered a gray steel bed frame. The only other fixtures were a toilet, a small table, and a chair. A locked metal door guaranteed he wouldn't leave.

It was a good thing he didn't have to stay here long, Dylan thought. His mom would come get him out of the detention center soon. That was what she always did. Again, he would be given a warning, but nothing would come of it.

Nearly an hour passed before a lady in a uniform came to Dylan's holding room. She was a short, dumpy-looking woman with shoes that clopped when she walked. Her hair wrapped behind her head into a bun and she wore a dress that hung to the middle of her shins like a tent. She looked like some kid's grandmother — probably was. She smiled sweetly as if welcoming him to some fancy hotel. "Your mom won't be coming down to get you until sometime tomorrow, so make yourself comfortable."

"What do you mean, tomorrow?"

The lady spoke sincerely. "Well, that means she won't be coming tonight, because if she came tonight, that wouldn't be tomorrow. Tomorrow means she is coming on a whole different day, the one after today."

"I know what tomorrow is!" Dylan snapped.

"Oh," the woman said, placing a surprised hand over her mouth, "I could have sworn you asked me what I meant by tomorrow. Please accept my apology."

Dylan kept his cool, but wished he could throw something at this human antique as she left the room. He would love to wipe that smug look off her face. The noise of her key locking the door sounded like the cocking of a rifle.

Dylan walked in angry circles. Why was everyone so uptight? He wondered about his mom. She could have gotten dressed and come right down. Maybe he had pushed her too far. But so what? If this was the straw that broke the camel's back, maybe it would be fun having a dead camel lying around.

As Dylan stared at the gray metal door, a knot tightened in his stomach. He had a bad feeling about this whole thing.

By the time his mom showed up the next day, it was almost noon. A deputy unlocked the door and stood waiting as Natalie entered the holding cell. After a night locked up alone, Dylan wanted to unload on her with every name he could think of, but held back. He was smart enough to know he should act really sorry. At least for a couple of days.

Today his mom was quiet, a pained expression making her eyes look tired. She just stood in the doorway and stared at him.

"Aren't you going to ask me why I did it?" Dylan asked.

"Oh, I already know why you did it," she said.

"And why is that?"

"Because you think Dylan Barstow is the only person living on the planet who has feelings. Nobody else matters."

"Mom, I was just out having a little fun," Dylan explained.

"And why is it that every time Dylan Barstow has fun, somebody else pays or gets hurt? I'm getting really tired of your fun."

"The world is getting too uptight," Dylan said, standing up. "Let's get out of this hole."

"You're not coming home today. I came late this morning because I've spent the last two hours trying to convince Mr. Krogan not to press charges. Lucky for you, he agreed, but only if you're kept far away from his cars. I also called your uncle Todd. He'll be flying in tomorrow to take you back to Oregon. You're spending the rest of the summer with him."

Dylan glanced at the deputy blocking the door as his

thoughts raced. Uncle Todd was his rich uncle who lived near Portland, Oregon. He looked like a bulldog on two feet. His neck came straight down from his ears to his massive shoulders. The guy still ran, lifted weights, and shaved his head almost bald, the same as when he was in the Marines.

"Why did you call him?" Dylan demanded. "I'm not going to Oregon for the rest of the summer."

"It's that or get tried in juvenile court. Maybe you don't quite understand how much trouble you're in. You committed a felony last night. I can only imagine what your father would have thought of this."

"Well, I guess we'll never know!" Dylan said, raising his voice. "He was too busy getting himself killed over in Timbuktu!"

Dylan's mother spoke slowly and deliberately. "We've talked about this before. Your father was a war correspondent in Darfur, in Sudan. He was covering the genocide of tens of thousands of people when he was killed. He knew the risks, but if he could have, he —"

"If he knew the risks," Dylan interrupted, "he shouldn't have been there."

"Is that what you were thinking when you climbed out your window and went for a joyride last night?" She fumbled for something in her purse. "Or do your own rules not apply to you?"

When Dylan failed to answer, his mother shook her head. "I want to show you something I hadn't planned on showing you until you were older." She took an envelope from her purse and handed it to Dylan.

"What's this?"

"It's one of the last letters your father sent to me before he was killed."

Dylan opened the envelope with its weird stamp and funny markings. He wasn't a very good reader. Slowly he unfolded the letter and let his eyes take in the page.

My Dear Natalie,

If anything should ever happen to me, know that I love you and Dylan more than life. I'm working here in Darfur because life has given me this chance to be a part of something bigger than myself: helping to stop the genocide of a nation's people. If I should ever get killed, it will be so that others might live. What I am doing may not seem as noble as fighting in war as a soldier, but this _is_ a battlefield, and I can contribute much. My weapons are my camera and my pen.

Please never let my devotion to this cause make you doubt my love for you and Dylan. I hope someday my son will understand the importance of sacrificing his own needs for the needs of another. I think of you both every morning when I wake and every night before I fall asleep. Hopefully I will be home soon.

All my love,

Sam

"He shouldn't have been there!" Dylan shouted, tossing the letter on the floor. He refused to make eye contact with his mother. He didn't want her to see his eyes tearing up.

Natalie stooped and picked it up. "You're not the center of the universe," she answered. "Sorry to be the one to tell you this. You're just not."

As Natalie turned to leave, Dylan raised his voice. "I'm not going to Oregon!"

She turned and shook her head. "You have no choice."

"I'll run away," Dylan shouted.

"Fine, then run away."

"You-you want me to?"

"No, I want you to be a decent human being. Somehow you think the world owes you something. Your father was the kindest person I've ever known, and you still have a mother who loves you more than anything. If you think that living on the streets will be better than spending the summer with your uncle, I can't stop you. I just don't want to be around when Todd finds you — and he will find you."

As his mother walked from the detention center, Dylan clenched his fists tightly. When his father died, it had hurt more than anybody could have known. Dad was the one person who understood. Mom tried, but Dad was the one who had liked his music, his skateboarding, and the writing that he never showed to anybody else, because they might laugh. He had never needed to protect his thoughts from Dad. He was like Zipper — he always listened. He never criticized.

But then he went and died.

Dylan didn't like feeling trapped, and right now he felt cornered. Having his mother afraid of what he might do had always been his ace in the hole. Now that card was disappearing and he didn't have any backup. He wasn't dumb enough to think that being on the streets would be any fun. Nor did he doubt his Uncle Todd would find him if he ran away. He would probably treat it like some high-tech mission with operatives and data searches. He'd probably use his connections to have the CIA or the FBI come after him. The man was a crazy war buff and still lived, talked, and dressed like he was in the military. Living with him would be like boot camp.

# CHAPTER 2

Nobody called or stopped by the rest of the day. It wasn't until the following afternoon that a deputy came and released Dylan, leading him to the front office. "You have two people waiting for you," he said.

Dylan drew in a deep breath, bracing himself. He didn't like it when he wasn't in control. He shoved his hands deep into his pockets, pushing his jeans so far down that his shirt no longer covered his underwear. His mom hated when he wore his pants this way.

Dylan first spotted his mother and then Uncle Todd. The two sat patiently in a waiting room to the side of the reception desk. Seeing him, they stood and came out to greet him. Dylan purposely shuffled his feet and walked slowly to show his disdain. This wasn't cool, what they were doing.

Uncle Todd extended his hand. "Hi, Dylan," he said. At first Dylan didn't return the handshake, but Uncle Todd kept his hand extended with a patient stare until Dylan reluctantly shook his hand. Uncle Todd's grip was like a vice. "Good to see you, son. It's been too long."

"I'm not your son," Dylan muttered.

Uncle Todd motioned him through the front door leading outside. "Let's go home."

---

Dylan felt like a caged animal with his uncle in the house.

"We'll be flying back to Portland tomorrow," Uncle Todd said, as if commenting on the weather. He handed Dylan a piece of paper. "You need to bring the following items if you have them. If not, we'll go shopping in Portland."

Dylan glanced at the long list: compass, mosquito spray, suntan lotion, hiking boots, sunglasses, light jeans, T-shirts, athletic socks, toothbrushes, and about a hundred other things. "Where are we going? On an expedition?"

"Actually, we are. We are going to Papua New Guinea. But I'll fill you in on that while we're flying to Portland." He handed Dylan two white tablets. "Here, take these while I'm thinking of it."

"What are they?"

"Malaria pills. Starting now, we need to take them every week until we get back. Now take them."

Dylan stood and put out his palm. Pills in hand, he retreated to the kitchen. "I need some water," he called back. When he reached the kitchen, he pretended to swallow the pills, but instead threw them in the garbage. He wasn't going on any expedition, and he wasn't going to take any weird medications. After his dad died, the guidance counselor at school had recommended that Dylan take some kind of pills to help with his depression. They just made him feel numb and empty. After a couple months of this, Dylan refused to take them. Adults were always trying to fix or change him, instead of just leaving him alone.

"What if I don't want to go to this Pa Pa Guinea Pig place?" Dylan asked, returning to the living room.

Uncle Todd sat watching television. "It's not negotiable," he said, not even looking up. "And get used to the name Papua New Guinea. You'll be seeing that place in your dreams by the time we're done. It will be your home for the summer. If it's easier, some people call the place PNG."

"Where is it, and why are we going there?"

"Like I said, I'll explain it all tomorrow, but roughly, PNG is on the other side of the planet." He glanced at his watch. "We better get some sleep. You still need to pack your bags, and we need to be up at O-five hundred to catch our flight."

As Dylan started up the stairs, Uncle Todd called out, "Your mom told me about your climbing out the window. Tonight that would be a huge mistake. Good night and sleep well."

Dylan replied by whistling. Zipper shot up the stairs from his favorite spot near the couch. Dylan entered his room and slammed the door. Falling to his knees, Dylan hugged Zipper. "Uncle Todd probably put a land mine on the porch roof, or rigged a trip wire to a hand grenade," Dylan said. "What can I do?"

Zipper wagged his tail.

One thing Dylan did know about his uncle was he wasn't one to bluff. He meant every word he said. Dylan stood and paced back and forth in his room, holding his head in his hands. It felt like his brains were going to explode.

Dylan knew he had no choice right now, so he would go along with this stupid PNG thing. But when the time was right, he would bail out. He wasn't anybody's puppet. Hands shaking with anger and frustration, Dylan packed his suitcase. He paid no attention to the list Uncle Todd had given him, but he made sure to throw in his music headset. His headphones helped him to tune out the world, and right now the world really needed tuning out.

That night, Dylan's constant tossing and turning crowded Zipper off the bed. Dylan dreamed he was running across a desert with a demon chasing him. Ahead he spotted a root cellar with an open door. The demon had almost caught him when, at the very last second, Dylan dove into the darkness and slammed the door closed. He turned the lock and ran to the far corner. Crouched on the floor in the dark, he watched in terror as the demon attacked the door. Dylan covered his ears to muffle the demon's screams. With each charge, the door splintered and began ripping from its hinges. Finally, with one last charge, the door crashed to the ground.

"Wakee wakee wakee," called the monster. "Get your butt out of bed. It's O-five hundred!"

Dylan woke with a start. Sitting up and breathing fast, he realized it was morning and Uncle Todd was standing in the doorway of his bedroom. "I'm awake," Dylan grumped, swinging his legs out of bed. It was still dark.

"Breakfast in ten minutes," Uncle Todd announced.

Dylan fumbled with his clothes, wishing he was back in the root cellar with the demon. By the time he dressed and dragged his suitcase downstairs, his mom had breakfast on the table. Uncle Todd sat sipping on a cup of hot coffee. "I'm not hungry," Dylan mumbled.

Uncle Todd motioned for him to sit. "This morning don't eat for yourself. It's not all about you."

"What are you talking about?"

"This morning you need to eat breakfast because your mother was kind enough to get up early and fix it for us."

Dylan looked to his mom but she avoided eye contact. For a moment he considered arguing, but Uncle Todd's intense gaze discouraged that. Grunting, Dylan slumped into a chair and began eating. He wouldn't have admitted it to his mother or Uncle Todd, but the scrambled eggs, hash browns, and bacon didn't taste half bad.

＿＿

As Dylan walked from the house that morning, he knelt and hugged Zipper good-bye. "I'm going to miss you, old boy," he whispered, blinking. A light rain fell, but that wasn't what made Dylan's eyes wet. With one last hug, he stood angrily and crawled into the car. He would have slammed the door but Uncle Todd was already holding it open for him, and closed it gently.

Nobody spoke much as they drove to the airport. Not until they pulled to a stop and climbed out did Natalie speak. "Dylan, I hope you have a good summer," she said, her voice wavering.

"You've already made sure that won't happen," Dylan snapped.

Suddenly his mother hugged him desperately. "Just know I love you."

Dylan stiffened, then pushed her away and pulled his suitcase from the trunk.

"Take good care of Zipper," he ordered, heading toward the terminal. He glanced back once and noticed that she was crying.

Uncle Todd caught up to Dylan as they approached the ticketing counter. "It doesn't take much of a man to be a jerk," he said.

Dylan ignored the comment, keeping to himself.

After clearing airport security and finding their gate, Uncle Todd finally turned to Dylan. "Okay, so here's what's happening. And the sooner you get aboard, the sooner this train leaves the station. Last winter, my father, your grandfather, Henry died. He had full-blown Alzheimer's disease. At the end, he had completely lost his memory and mind. During the Second World War, Henry was a B-17 bomber pilot and was shot down over Papua New Guinea. He never spoke of his war years. After Dad died, I was executor of his estate and in charge of cleaning out the old farmhouse down near Grants Pass. When I was cleaning, I found this in the attic."

Uncle Todd reached into his upper jacket pocket and pulled out a small leather-bound notebook. He handed it to Dylan. "This is a journal your grandfather kept during the months and weeks leading up to the day they were shot down. Five crew members survived the initial crash, but three died the first night. In the end, your grandfather was the only survivor. He was lost for two weeks in the jungle before being found by natives, badly dehydrated and burning up with fever from malaria and gangrene.

"The military searched for the wreckage but never found it. Jungles in PNG are so dense, thousands of planes crashed during the war and were never seen again."

"Why did so many planes crash?" Dylan asked.

"The air war against Japan to protect Australia was fought over Papua New Guinea. Most of the planes that crashed were shot down, but there was also bad weather, horrible maps with uncharted mountains, no radar or guidance systems, and a thousand other problems. It was hell. By the end of the war, more planes were lost in PNG than in any other country in the world. So many soldiers died that even today, after heavy rains, skeletons float up in the swamps."

"Cool," Dylan said, leafing through the handwritten journal. At a glance, it was all about missions, weather, bad living conditions, and missing home. He handed the journal back to his uncle.

"No, keep it. I want you to read every word," Uncle Todd said. "That journal actually survived the crash and your grandfather's two weeks in the jungle. I am convinced that somewhere in those pages we can find enough clues to help us finally find the wreckage. That's where we're going for the summer. We're going to join three other searchers. Our group will try to find your grandfather's B-17 bomber. The plane's name was *Second Ace*."

Dylan shrugged. "What can be so hard about finding some plane? We'll just get in a jeep and drive around looking for it."

Uncle Todd laughed aloud. "Papua New Guinea has everything from jungles and swamps to fourteen-thousand-foot peaks. It has some of the most unforgiving real estate on the planet. During the war, there were crews that crashed three miles from the airport. It took them more than a week to hack their way through the jungle with machetes to safety — and they knew where they were going. In some parts of the jungle, you can't see wreckage fifty feet away."

Dylan slumped down in his seat and put on his headphones. "This is really a dumb idea," he said, shutting his eyes and turning up the volume. The music hadn't even started when the headphones were pulled from his ears. He opened his eyes to find his uncle staring at him intensely.

"Hey, what did you do that for?" Dylan demanded.

"You need to read the journal so you can be part of the team. Every member has an obligation to every other member to be as knowledgeable as possible. It may save a life."

"I don't care if we find some dumb bomber."

Uncle Todd handed the headphones back. "You don't care much about anything."

"Okay, I'll read the journal, but I can still listen to music while I'm reading."

Uncle Todd shook his head. "You won't need your headphones anymore. You use them to tune out the world, and this summer is all about discovering the world."

Dylan hesitated, tempted to defy his uncle.

"Put them away, or I'll put them away for you," Uncle Todd said plainly.

Reluctantly Dylan opened the small leather journal and began to read, feeling the stare of his Uncle Todd.

June 21, 1942

Arrived in Papua New Guinea at the Jackson Airstrip at 0900 this morning. Was greeted by the commander with these words: "Welcome, gentlemen. This island is plagued with malaria, dengue fever, diarrhea, dysentery, and every other tropical disease known to man. If you are shot down and survive, do not start a fire unless you want to be caught. Always save one extra round of ammunition for yourself if you are captured by either the Japanese, cannibals, or headhunters. None will let you live. Headhunters will cut off your head. The Japanese will torture you and then kill you. And cannibals, just like in the movies, will roast you over

A FIRE ON A POLE AND EAT YOU. YOU TASTE A LITTLE LIKE CHICKEN.

"AVOIDING THE ENEMY IS THE LEAST OF YOUR PROBLEMS. WE HAVE TWO KINDS OF WEATHER, BAD AND WORSE. THERE ARE PLENTY OF SNAKES AND LIZARDS OVER TEN FEET IN LENGTH. BUGS ARE EVERYWHERE, SOME THE SIZE OF SMALL BIRDS THAT SUCK BODY FLUIDS FROM YOU WHILE YOU SLEEP. IF YOU DIE IN THE JUNGLE, RATS WILL PICK YOUR BONES CLEAN WITHIN DAYS. DON'T THINK WAR IS GLORIOUS. IT AIN'T.

"IF YOU MAKE IT OUT OF THE JUNGLE TO A RIVER, MOST RIVERS ARE THICK WITH CROCODILES. ONCE YOU GET TO THE OCEAN, THE SHARKS ARE JUST AS THICK. WAR IS SERIOUS BUSINESS AND IS NOT FOR NICE PEOPLE. YOU WILL NOT HAVE SECOND CHANCES.

"NOW, GET YOUR TRENCHES DUG QUICKLY. THE ENEMY ALREADY KNOWS YOU'RE HERE AND WE WILL BE UNDER FULL ATTACK IN TWO HOURS. ENJOY YOUR STAY!"

Dylan turned to Uncle Todd. "Do they still have cannibals in this New Guinea place?"

Uncle Todd nodded. "Twenty-seven of them were arrested just last week." He smirked. "Kind of brings new meaning to 'having a friend for dinner.'" Still chuckling, he added, "This summer, our biggest problem will be all the bugs and insects." He motioned to the loading gate. "It's time for us to board."

When they were settled on the plane, Dylan caught his

uncle watching him. Reluctantly he picked up the journal again. The next entry was written three days after the first.

JUNE 24, 1942

THIS IS AN UGLY PLACE. THE FIRST NIGHT WE ARRIVED, I THOUGHT THE FULL TROPICAL MOON WAS PRETTY. NOW I'M CUSSING IT. FULL MOONS ARE WHEN THE ENEMY BOMBERS COME. ALREADY WE HAVE BEEN UNDER TWO BOMBING ATTACKS AND HAVE NOT FLOWN A SINGLE MISSION. LAST NIGHT I SAW MY FIRST CASUALTY, A YOUNG SERGEANT BLOWN IN HALF BY ONE OF THE BOMBS THAT DROPPED. I HELPED CARRY HIS LEGS TO THE GRAVE WE DUG.

THE GREASE MONKEYS ARE STILL WORKING ON OUR PLANES. MAINTENANCE IS A JOKE. THERE ARE NO HANGARS, TOOLS, OR SPARE PARTS. WE HAVE WHAT WE LANDED WITH. AS OF RIGHT NOW, WE ARE LOSING THE WAR HERE. IF WE FAIL TO STOP THE JAPANESE, THEY WILL TAKE OVER ALL OF NEW GUINEA AND THE NORTHERN HALF OF AUSTRALIA. THE ENEMY IS ONLY SIX MILES UP THE TRAIL FROM US. A SNIPER IS PROBABLY WATCHING ME WRITE THIS ENTRY. OUR SHIPS LOAD AND UNLOAD AT NIGHT, HIDING AT SEA DURING THE DAY. WAR IS TOUGH.

Dylan read several more entries before realizing that Uncle Todd was still watching him. "What are you staring at?" Dylan asked.

"I'm trying to figure out how somebody who has had

everything handed to him on a silver platter could ever think the world owes him anything."

"I don't think that," Dylan said.

Uncle Todd shrugged. "Something else must be getting under your skin, then," he said. "You have a chip on your shoulder as big as a log."

To escape Uncle Todd's icy stare, Dylan looked back down at the journal.

July 1, 1942

STILL HAVE NOT FLOWN A MISSION. EVERY DAY WE TRY TO MAKE OURSELVES BUSY HELPING THE GREASE MONKEYS WORK ON OUR BOMBERS OR DIGGING OUR TRENCHES DEEPER. I WENT THROUGH MY SURVIVAL KIT YESTERDAY AND ADDED A FEW THINGS. I NOW HAVE A PISTOL AND PLENTY OF AMMUNITION, A SHARP KNIFE, GAS MASK, FIRST-AID KIT, MIRROR, MOSQUITO NETTING, FISH HOOKS, AND SOME EXTRA RATIONS AND WATER TO STORE IN THE COCKPIT IN CASE WE CRASH-LAND. THIS PLACE IS UNLIKE ANY I HAVE EVER SEEN.

THERE ARE NO BUILDINGS HERE AT JACKSON AIRSTRIP EXCEPT A SMALL TOWER THAT IS BEING BUILT. EVERYTHING IS DONE IN THE OPEN, RAIN OR SHINE, DAY OR NIGHT, SEVEN DAYS A WEEK. WE ARE NOW OFFICIALLY IN THE BOONDOCKS.

Dylan's eyes had grown heavy and his head fell forward as he drifted into a deep sleep. Somewhere in the distance he thought he heard drum beats. He dreamed he had wings and was flying toward the sound. The drumming grew louder as he spotted smoke drifting upward like a ribbon of white from the jungle. Gliding closer, Dylan could see that the smoke billowed from a big fire. Tied to a pole and being roasted over the fire like a hotdog on a stick was a white-skinned boy named Dylan Barstow.

Dylan wasn't sure he liked the taste of chicken anymore.

# CHAPTER 3

There wasn't much to talk about as the Boeing 737 took off. This was only Dylan's second ride in an airplane. His first had been when he was eight and his dad was still alive. They flew to Florida. While other kids enjoyed Disney World, his father, Sam, dragged him through mangrove swamps in the everglades looking for rare birds and alligators. And when they did go to an amusement park, it had to be Epcot, the more adult part of Disney World. At least they got to ride the Mission: SPACE flight simulator. Dylan had loved it. His mom screamed the whole ride and almost got sick from the G-force.

Dylan sat by the window and stared out at the shore of Lake Michigan passing under the wing. He fingered the journal as he stared out the window. He didn't like reading about waking up with spiders, being attacked by the Japanese, and keeping the crew's morale up, but finally, out of boredom, he opened the small leather journal to read more.

July 8, 1942

TODAY WE FLEW OUR FIRST MISSION. THE LANDING STRIP HERE AT JACKSON AIRSTRIP IS SCARY. IT'S LIKE LANDING AND

TAKING OFF FROM A POSTAGE STAMP. NOT A GOOD PLACE FOR AN OVERLOADED BOMBER WITH A FULL CREW. WE FLEW A BOMBING MISSION OVER LAE LOOKING FOR SHIPS AND ANTI-AIRCRAFT ARTILLERY SITES. WE BRIEFED OUR MISSION FOR 26,000 FEET WITH THREE OTHER B-17s. I THOUGHT THE HIGH-ALTITUDE COLD WOULD BE WELCOME, BUT IT WAS BITTER. MY OXYGEN MASK KEPT FREEZING UP. I FINALLY SWITCHED TO A PORTABLE FOR TEN MINUTES AFTER THE BOMB DROP. TWO JAPANESE ZEROS MADE A RUN ON US BUT WE HAD THE ADVANTAGE OF ALTITUDE AND THE SUN AT OUR BACKS. MY BALL TURRET GUNNER CLAIMED HE SAW SMOKE FROM ONE OF THE ZEROS BEFORE THEY TURNED TAIL TO RUN. SECOND ACE AND THE OTHER B-17s RETURNED WITHOUT DAMAGE. THINK WE KNOCKED OUT ONE OF THE AAA GUN SITES.

I UNDERSTAND NOW WHY THEY SAY, "NEVER PASS UP A MEAL, BECAUSE YOU DON'T KNOW WHEN OR IF THERE WILL BE A NEXT ONE."

Reading the journal made Dylan think about his dad. Had Dad ever written a journal like this? Mom showed him the one letter, but surely there were others. Suddenly Dylan wanted to know more about his father. What had it been like in Darfur? Dylan clenched his fists. If he was still in Wisconsin, he could have asked Mom about it. That was where he should be right now. Not stuck on some airplane with his uncle, flying to Oregon. What else would Uncle Todd think of to make life more miserable than it already was?

"Stupid," Dylan whispered under his breath, as Lake Michigan drifted away behind the wing.

———

They changed planes in Minneapolis and flew on to Portland. Uncle Todd had his car parked at the airport. Dylan hadn't known that his uncle drove a red Corvette. It was an antique 1962 Vette with the old-style rounded headlights and Stingray back. It had a hardtop that could come off in good weather. Dylan tried not to show his excitement.

Uncle Todd caught Dylan staring and smiled. "Back in high school, you could buy one of these in cherry condition for less than two thousand dollars," he said.

"How much do they cost now?" Dylan asked.

"I've seen them for way over fifty thousand."

"Must be nice having money," Dylan said.

"I'm surprised I still have a butt," Uncle Todd said.

"What do you mean?"

"I worked my butt off earning every penny I ever had. That's what makes it so great now. People who have things given to them never appreciate it." When Dylan didn't answer, Uncle Todd spoke again. "We won't be leaving for almost two weeks. Maybe you can drive this thing before we leave."

"No way — I don't have a license."

Uncle Todd grinned. "That didn't stop you before."

Dylan chuckled.

"I know where there's an abandoned parking lot south of here. That would be a good place."

"So how come you agreed to take me for the summer?" Dylan asked.

"Your dad, Sam, was my brother — it's what he would have wanted." Uncle Todd paused. "And I agree with your mom."

"Agree with what?"

"That you're a good person inside, if you ever take the time to find that person. Right now he's buried under a pile of anger. You're trying to prove something to yourself, and I haven't quite figured out yet what you're trying to prove."

"I'm not trying to prove anything," Dylan snapped. He hated being analyzed.

"Yes, you are. Just because Dylan Barstow says something with his mouth doesn't mean tiddly-dink as far as the truth. You should know that by now."

Dylan bit his tongue. His uncle was always so sure of himself. He had his own front he was keeping up for some reason. Why did he still live all alone and act like a drill sergeant?

They drove the rest of the way in silence. When Uncle Todd pulled up to his condo in Gresham, a town east of Portland, he revved the engine, then turned the key to OFF.

"Welcome to my world," he said. "We get a lot of rain here. Today it's sunny, so let's make use of it. Grab your stuff and I'll show you where your room is. Then we're going running."

"That's all right," Dylan said. "I don't like to run."

"Excuse me, did I say, 'Can we run?' Did I say, 'Would you like to take a little jog, Your Royal Highness?' Maybe we need to get something straight right up front. The reason you're here is because you've been making bad choices. This summer I make the choices. Is there anything about that program that you don't understand?" When Dylan didn't answer, Uncle Todd added, "Let's get you settled and then I'll meet you down here for a run in thirty minutes." Without waiting for an answer, Uncle Todd headed into the house, not even offering to carry Dylan's heavy suitcase.

---

The run turned out to be more than a jog. They ran five miles, as if it were the Boston Marathon. "Why do we have to run so fast?" Dylan complained, struggling to keep up.

"Because if we wanted to go slow, we'd have brought wheelchairs. I'm almost sixty years old. What are you — a fossil?"

Dylan didn't like being called a fossil. He ran out ahead of Uncle Todd until they returned home, where he collapsed on the grass. "Why do we have to go running?" Dylan gasped, breathing hard.

"When we get to Papua New Guinea, we'll be doing some serious hiking. We won't have time to get into shape then. You'll be thanking me for this when we get there. We have exactly two weeks to get you as strong as we can."

They headed inside and Dylan flopped onto the couch. He wouldn't be thanking Uncle Todd for anything. He was still trying to figure out how to get out of even going to this dumb PNG place. He had yet to figure out any plan. Just being here with Uncle Todd was Dylan's worst nightmare — his summer from hell!

"Go shower and get cleaned up. We're going out for pizza," Uncle Todd ordered.

"I'm not hungry," Dylan said.

"And I'm not a giraffe. But we're still going out for pizza. So, HOP! HOP!" Uncle Todd clapped his hands for emphasis.

Dylan wanted to scream as he shuffled slowly up the steps to his room.

———

He would never have admitted it to his uncle, but Dylan felt good for having run five miles, and he slept like a baby that night. He could have slept another five hours when he heard the dreaded "Wakee wakee wakee!" at six the next morning.

"We don't have any plane to catch," Dylan pleaded.

"No, but there is a new day out there waiting for us to get our butts out of bed. It's already light out. If you beat me this morning, I'll take you to Perkins for breakfast. I beat you, we come back here for some of my cooking. I suggest you try and beat me."

In ten minutes, they were running down the empty street.

"Let's jog to warm up," Uncle Todd said, "and then we'll see how fast Dylan Barstow can really run. Yesterday I took it easy on you."

Before they reached the end of the block, Uncle Todd reached over and nudged Dylan's arm. "Same route as yesterday, down around the park and then home." He shouted "Go!" and quickened his pace.

There was no way Dylan was going to let this arrogant old man beat him in a footrace. It didn't matter that he was a human bulldog. Knowing how he felt yesterday, running all out, Dylan paced himself, not even trying to get ahead of Uncle Todd. He could pass him anytime he wanted, but for now, let the old geezer think he was winning.

Soon they had rounded the park and were headed home. Dylan still hung back, waiting until he knew he could sprint to the finish. But as they neared home, Dylan realized he wouldn't be sprinting anywhere. Just keeping up with Uncle Todd had become a struggle. By the time they were a block from home, Dylan's legs felt like rubber. Still, he ran faster. Each pounding step felt like it was his last. At half a block he was even with his uncle. A hundred yards away, he was still even. Fifty feet away, they were running down the middle of the street. He closed his eyes and willed himself to run harder than he had ever run in his life. When he opened his eyes to angle up the drive, he was only inches ahead of Uncle Todd, but he was ahead!

Pumping his arms in the air, he collapsed on the grass. "I'm going to eat a whole cow at Perkins," Dylan panted.

Uncle Todd smiled, gasping for air himself. He bent at the waist, hands on his knees, as he struggled to catch his breath. "Now that's the Dylan I like and the Dylan I remember," he exclaimed. He caught several more breaths, and then continued. "You ran smart, pacing yourself. I thought you would run like a bonehead and try to be ahead of me from the beginning, but you didn't. And at the end, you had willpower. A lot of kids don't. You made me proud, and now you don't have to eat my cooking. You lucky stiff!"

For the moment, Dylan forgot his situation and grinned. He had just beaten Uncle Todd in an all-out footrace. He even got a compliment out of the old fart. His uncle extended his hand to help him up, and Dylan allowed himself to be pulled to his feet.

———

Sitting in Perkins waiting for their orders, Uncle Todd folded his cloth napkin back and forth. "By the way," he said. "If you want to call your mother, feel free any time."

"Why would I want to call her?" Dylan said. "She's the one that got me into this mess."

"No, you're the one that got you into this mess. Don't blame her."

"Whatever," Dylan said.

" 'Whatever' — you know what that means, don't you?"

"What?"

"That's code for 'screw you.' You're telling me my words aren't important."

"Is there anything I can do that isn't wrong?"

"It's not what you do, it's why you do it," Uncle Todd said. After a pause, he continued. "Look, you can live, dress, talk, do anything you want, if it's to be different. If you want to stand out, be comfortable, be noticed, be stylish, I'm okay with that. But from what I've seen, you don't blow your nose without attitude. Escaping with your headset, wearing your pants low, saying 'whatever' — you do all of those things to thumb your nose at people and be disrespectful.

"I dress and act a lot different than you, but nothing I say or do is meant to be disrespectful of you. I expect the same respect back. Maybe you got away treating your mom without respect. Now you're on a different planet."

"I don't do those things to be disrespectful," Dylan argued.

Uncle Todd shook his head and snickered.

"What's so funny?" Dylan asked.

"You," Uncle Todd said. "You think because your mouth says something, the whole world believes you. You're so angry that everything you do is to show your contempt. Treat me that way and we have a problem. Understand?" When Dylan didn't answer, Uncle Todd raised his voice and said,

"Do the respectful thing and answer my question. Do we understand each other?"

People in other booths were now staring over at them. Knowing there would be no escaping Uncle Todd, Dylan nodded. He wanted to say, "Whatever," but instead mumbled, "Yes."

# CHAPTER 4

Each day with Uncle Todd became a bigger challenge. At home there had been a thousand ways that Dylan could get away with doing as he pleased. Here, he lived under a microscope. Every move, every word, every twitch of his muscles was analyzed. Dylan felt like a lab rat. And every morning they ran, even in the rain. Dylan made sure he beat Uncle Todd running. That was the single thing that brought him any satisfaction. But finally, even that lost its appeal.

One morning, a week after arriving in Oregon, Uncle Todd shouted "Go!" and sped up. Dylan didn't respond. Instead he kept trotting along slowly at the pace they had warmed up at. Uncle Todd looked back but then kept running. Dylan hadn't even reached the park when his uncle passed him, returning to the house. "See you at the house," he called. "I'm cooking this morning."

"Whatever," Dylan muttered. This was stupid, running in the rain.

—

By the time Dylan returned home, Uncle Todd had breakfast fixed. "Let's eat before we shower," he said. "Breakfast is ready."

Dylan slumped into a chair at the table, actually hungry.

"Here," Uncle Todd said, placing burned toast and a bowl of mystery mush in front of him. The mush was some kind of white slop that looked like oatmeal but was more grainy. "What is this?" Dylan asked.

"Those are grits," Uncle Todd announced proudly. "My favorite breakfast."

Dylan knew better than to refuse the meal, but he had to swallow each bite quickly to keep from puking. If this was someone's favorite breakfast, they were some kind of sick. Finally, swallowing the last gross mouthful of mush, Dylan stood. "I'm going up to shower."

"You can shower after telling me you appreciated me making breakfast, and after taking this." Uncle Todd handed Dylan another malaria pill.

Dylan lost it. "But I didn't like the breakfast," he snapped. "It tasted like crap!"

"Then say thank you out of respect. You don't have to like something to be respectful."

Feeling cornered, Dylan finally mumbled, "Thanks."

"Good," Uncle Todd said. "After we clean up, let's go drive the Corvette. If you're still up to it."

Dylan hid his excitement. "That would be okay," he said, shrugging. "Won't it be better if it's not raining?"

Uncle Todd shook his head. "With what we're doing this morning, rain is actually better for learning."

Bounding up the stairs, Dylan pumped his fists with excitement. He was getting to drive his first Corvette. Before showering, he flushed the malaria pill down the toilet.

———

As they drove back toward Portland, Uncle Todd explained their plan. "The place where we're going is a huge parking lot by a factory that has been closed down. Our car club has permission to go there. We'll use pylons to practice maneuvering. Ever heard of drifting?"

"As in like a snowdrift?"

"No, as in like controlled power sliding with a car."

Dylan shook his head.

Soon they pulled off the main highway and drove through an industrial subdivision for another mile. Finally they pulled up to a locked gate. Uncle Todd crawled from the red Corvette and unlocked the door.

"Is this legal?" Dylan ventured as Uncle Todd crawled back behind the wheel.

Uncle Todd nodded. "You don't mind doing something if it's legal, do you?"

"Just wondering."

Soon they circled behind a big building with almost a quarter mile of loading docks. Except for a few phone poles, the parking lot was a huge open expanse of concrete. Already highway cones marked a large course. "Okay, let me show you what we're going to do," Uncle Todd said. "Start out slow and then go faster."

"I'm not afraid to go fast," Dylan said.

"You should be — that's how people kill themselves," Uncle Todd said, downshifting. "There's no fools in this car, unless you know of one. First let me show you what happens if we do things wrong."

Uncle Todd sped up and headed out onto the small track created by the plastic pylons. As he steered into the first corner, Dylan knew they were going too fast to make the corner, especially on wet pavement. "You're going too fast," he said loudly.

As they entered the corner, the car spun out. The Corvette left the course, sliding backward until it came to a slow stop.

"I knew we were going too fast," Dylan bragged.

"We were going exactly thirty miles per hour — too fast for someone who doesn't know their butt from a banana. Now watch this." Uncle Todd shifted and drove around until he approached the corner again. "We're going thirty miles per hour again," he commented.

"And we're still going too fast," Dylan said.

"You would sure think so, wouldn't you?" Uncle Todd answered smugly.

Just as they entered the corner, Uncle Todd shifted down hard and hit the gas pedal as if to speed up. Was he crazy? The car began sliding, but this time Uncle Todd steered sharply in the opposite direction, away from the turn. As if held by a huge hand, the car drifted magically around the corner, turning at a sideways angle almost the whole way.

"This is drifting," Uncle Todd said. "A Corvette isn't the ideal car to use, but it's okay because it has rear-wheel drive. Racers use this technique all the time so they don't have to slow down for a corner."

"Can I try it?" Dylan exclaimed.

Uncle Todd nodded. "First I want you to practice a few things. We'll start by cutting donuts — you have experience with that."

"That's easy," Dylan said.

"We'll see," Uncle Todd said. "The night you broke into the junkyard, I'll bet this is how you cut your donuts." Uncle Todd floored the gas pedal and cranked the steering wheel to the left. Soon the car spun its tires on the wet pavement and rotated around in circles as if the front bumper was glued to a post. Uncle Todd leaned casually against the door and looked over at Dylan. As the Corvette continued to whip in circles, Uncle Todd said, "See, this is simple. Any knucklehead can get a car to do this." He winked. "Even in a plowed field. But now let's make the donut bigger."

Instead of keeping the steering wheel cranked left into the turn, Uncle Todd turned the wheel to the right and let up slightly on the gas pedal. Slowly the car quit spinning around its front bumper and started to drift forward. "Okay, I'm going to keep the steering wheel just like this to the right, but

I'm going to control my drift and the size of our circle with only the gas pedal. Watch."

Dylan stared in amazement as the Corvette drifted in a bigger and bigger circle.

"Okay, I'm letting off on the power even more. Watch this." The car drifted into a bigger circle, but still to the left, nearly sideways. The steering wheel was cranked in the opposite direction. As if sitting comfortably in a lounge chair, Uncle Todd spoke casually. "I control everything with power, shifting, and steering. It's a fine balance that takes years of practice and skill. It's easier on wet pavement because you don't have to use as much power or speed. It doesn't wear the tires as much, and it's easier to practice. Are you ready to try?"

All of a sudden, Dylan wasn't so sure of himself. This wasn't as easy as he had thought. What if he screwed it up? What if he flipped the car? This was no longer a reckless joyride in a junked car. Swallowing his apprehension, Dylan traded seats and pulled his seat belt tight. "Okay, what do I do first?" he asked, his voice shaking.

"Get rid of your pride. Inside this car, no one is trying to show off, be cool, or prove anything. All you're doing today is learning. Drive around some, changing your speed and going through the gears to get used to the power. This isn't a junkyard now."

"Do you have to keep reminding me about that?" Dylan said.

"I hope you never forget. Now get used to the car."

Dylan obeyed. After a few minutes driving around and testing the controls and shift, he felt comfortable.

"Okay, now shift into first and go about ten miles per hour."

When Dylan was ready, Uncle Todd said, "Now crank the steering wheel all the way to the left and keep adding power until you're spinning donuts."

Dylan felt a huge lump in his throat. This car was no wreck from a junkyard. He was driving a fifty-thousand-dollar classic Corvette. If he wrecked this thing, it would really prove that he was a big screw-up. Carefully he cranked the wheel until the car began spinning in circles to the left.

"Add some power," Uncle Todd reminded him.

As Dylan added power, the car spun faster and faster, its front end holding to the inside.

"Okay, now crank your wheels all the way to the right. If you start to straighten out, don't let off the gas. Add power!"

Dylan sucked in a deep breath and cranked the wheel right. This went against everything his brain told him. You didn't add power and steer to the right to make bigger circles to the left. But that was exactly what he was doing, and as if by magic, the red Corvette started carving larger circles to the left on the wet pavement.

"Your power is overriding your steering," Uncle Todd said calmly, his voice as casual as if he were explaining where the milk was in the refrigerator. "Keep it just like this until you feel comfortable with what's happening."

After the car had made five or six big circles, Uncle Todd said, "Okay, now back off a little on the power and make an even bigger circle. If you have to, steer a little to keep from spinning or going straight."

Dylan obeyed, and soon found himself struggling to keep the high-powered Corvette under control.

"Okay, make the circle tighter again," Uncle Todd said.

Scrambling to think, Dylan slowly pushed on the gas pedal and felt the car start to drift more. He purposely oversteered as the car slowed and slid nearly sideways into a tighter turn.

"This is awesome!" Dylan exclaimed.

After half an hour of practicing, Dylan felt like he had run a marathon. Sweat dripped from every pore of his body, and his arm muscles cramped. This was way harder than spinning donuts in some farmer's field.

Finally, Uncle Todd said, "Okay, that's enough for today. Tomorrow, we'll practice this some more, and maybe practice entering a drift going faster."

Dylan was thankful the day's practice had ended. This hadn't been as easy as he had expected. Driving a powerful car this way was super hard. His body trembled as he stopped the Vette and let Uncle Todd back in the driver's seat.

"Thanks," he said.

"You did a good job," Uncle Todd said. "A few more years of practice and we'll have you driving sprint cars on some dirt track."

"Maybe I should stick to farmers' fields," Dylan said.

"I was hoping to get you away from that," Uncle Todd said, grinning. "Let's go get us some cheeseburgers."

As they drove off the big lot and out of the industrial complex, Dylan struggled with his feelings. On one hand he was still mad at his mom and Uncle Todd and at the stupid world. On the other hand, he wished all of the boys at school back home could have seen screw-up Dylan Barstow today drifting an expensive Corvette.

# CHAPTER 5

The next morning, running in pouring rain, Dylan made sure to beat his uncle — he didn't ever want to eat burned toast and grits again. As they finished breakfast at Perkins, Uncle Todd informed Dylan, "I have someplace I want to take you today. We're driving up to Vancouver."

"What for?" Dylan asked.

"You'll see."

Uncle Todd's surprises made Dylan nervous. With the rain still heavy, they drove the Corvette north from Portland. Even when they pulled into a nursing home called Garden Acres, Dylan still didn't know what was happening.

"There's somebody I want you to meet. His name is Frank Bower. Frank flew twenty-five missions during the war."

"I've skipped school more times than that," Dylan bragged.

Uncle Todd gave Dylan one of his "you just said something stupid" looks. "During the war, the average number of missions flown before you were killed was seven," Uncle Todd said.

"Seven?" Dylan said. "That's suicide!"

Uncle Todd nodded. "Thousands of young men risked their lives so you and I could live as free people. Their regular missions were bad, and their bad missions were hell. Not many survived. Because of that, there aren't many of these old guys still living. I called up Frank and asked him if he would tell you about some of his missions, and he agreed. He was a waist gunner on a B-17 in Europe during the Second World War. Waist gunners shot machine guns out the sides of bombers at attacking fighters."

Dylan didn't really want to go hear some old guy talk about being in the war, but he knew he had no choice. He shrugged and almost said, "Whatever," but then bit his tongue and said nothing. Reluctantly he followed Uncle Todd into a nursing home filled with old people sitting in wheelchairs. Some wandered about with long-distance stares like zombies.

"This place freaks me out," Dylan mumbled.

"Someday we'll all be this age," Uncle Todd said. "Native Americans revered elders instead of throwing them away. Every person here has a story to tell. If you knew their past, you would want to talk to every one of them."

"Doubt that," Dylan said as he followed Uncle Todd.

Nobody was at the receptionist's desk, so they walked down the hallway to the nurses' station. A red-haired nurse greeted them and pointed them to the lounge, where they found an old man with a blue flannel shirt sitting near a window, staring out.

"Frank, how you doing?" Uncle Todd said loudly, announcing their arrival.

The old man turned his head and smiled. "I'm still breathing, if that tells you anything."

Dylan glanced around. He really didn't like being here. The old people made him feel like he was in some nuthouse. The smell in the air was like somebody had sprayed perfume in a bathroom after a bad fart.

Uncle Todd pulled up two chairs. "This is my nephew, Dylan. He's going with me to Papua New Guinea to help me look for that B-17, *Second Ace*, the one I told you about. I thought it would be great for him to hear right from the horse's mouth what it was like being a waist gunner during the war."

"You'll have to forgive me if sometimes I have a short circuit between my ears," Frank Bower said. The thin, silver-haired man laughed aloud at his wit, then explained. "I can tell you how many cows my dad milked during the blizzard of 1932, but sometimes I can't even remember my middle name. Time and war have scrambled my brain. I'll remember what I can. Did your uncle tell you I flew twenty-five missions?"

Dylan nodded. "He said most crews only lived through seven."

The old man nodded. "You already know more than most people. If you flew twenty-five missions, you got to go home. We called it the 'Lucky Bastards' Club.' Every crew member wanted to join that club, but most weren't lucky enough bastards." Again Frank laughed, then looked down at his lap. He twisted at his shirt with gnarly hands. His fingers had big knuckles. "You ever smelled death?" he asked Dylan, looking up suddenly.

Dylan really didn't like sitting here being questioned by this old codger, but the man's riveting glare couldn't be avoided. "Y-you mean like a dead cat?" Dylan stammered.

"I mean like your best friend drowning in his own blood as you hold him in your arms."

Dylan scuffed his shoes on the floor and looked out the window to avoid the old guy's stare.

"Most of my missions were in a B-17 called *Miss Audrey*. On my third mission over Germany, my ball turret gunner, Jamie, took a twenty-millimeter round through the stomach. It didn't kill him right away. His beating heart kept him conscious for about ten minutes, the longest ten minutes of my life. Bled all over everything.

"They could never wash away the blood, and I didn't like flying in *Miss Audrey* after that, 'cause she always had the smell of death. This wasn't a Hollywood movie. When you died, you really died." Frank stared out the window as if remembering, but then shook his head. "Uh, where was I?"

"You were talking about your crew members," Uncle Todd said.

"Yeah, well, our crew, we were a family. I still remember the boys like brothers. Big Sam, the pilot. Andy, the copilot.

Billy, the navigator. The bombardier, a farm boy called Luther. Mosley, the tail gunner. I was a waist gunner. The other waist gunner was Max. After Jamie died, we got another ball turret gunner. We called him Shorty, 'cause he was small enough to fit down in the ball turret. The top turret gunner was Sonny. Luke was the radio operator."

"Did you ever want to be a pilot?" Uncle Todd asked.

Frank shook his head. "If I'm going duck hunting, I don't want to row the boat." Frank laughed and coughed at his own joke. "What else do you want to know?"

"If it was so dangerous, why did you join the air force?" Dylan asked, his voice accusing.

"I guess I joined because I was patriotic, and at the beginning it was this great adventure, being flown across the Atlantic Ocean. We were stationed in England and drank warm beer in pubs with guys who talked with funny accents. We ate weird foods and drove on the wrong side of the road in fog as thick as soup. But the main reason we were there was to stop a madman called Hitler from taking over the world. After that mission when Jamie died in my arms, it wasn't patriotism anymore. It was revenge, and we were just trying to stay alive." Frank shifted in his wheelchair. "Let me explain something. I was twenty-two years old when I enlisted. Most of the boys were just kids, barely eighteen years old. But if you survived the war, you returned as a man who had been to hell and back."

When Frank quit talking again, Uncle Todd asked, "Did you know the other crews?"

"We didn't hang out much with the other crews, because your drinking buddy today would probably be the body bag you helped unload tomorrow. And the Japanese and Germans weren't our only enemies. The wretched weather killed a lot of us."

"Was that your worst mission, when Jamie got killed?" Uncle Todd asked.

Frank shook his head. "My worst mission was my last mission."

"Did you ever get hurt?" Dylan ventured.

"Sure did. But not as bad as Sonny and Mosley."

"What happened?"

"You don't want to hear that story."

"We do," Uncle Todd insisted.

Frank turned to Dylan. "You want to hear that story, too, kid?"

Dylan didn't like being called "kid," but he managed a nod. "I guess."

Frank took a deep breath, as if to prepare himself for something very difficult. "Like I said, my mind ain't so good anymore, but some things you never forget. Cold dark mornings getting up before a mission, looking back into the barracks wondering how many bunks would be empty by nightfall. Breakfast. Suiting up. Briefings. Jeep rides down the flight line to the bomber. The rumble of takeoff. Seeing hundreds of planes, all in formation. The shaking of the bomber as our fifty-caliber machine guns fought off fighters. Anti-aircraft flak thudding around us, thicker than fireworks at a Fourth of July party. The 'bombs away' call over the intercom. The quiet flight home wondering how many crews had died that day. The shot of whiskey the brass always gave us during debriefing to calm our nerves — I can tell you it was never enough to wash away the hurt of missing crews. Then we had to get ready for the next day's mission." Frank turned and stared out the window. "Yup, it was rough," he mumbled.

After several minutes, Uncle Todd prodded some. "What happened on that last mission?"

Frank shook his head as if clearing away cobwebs. "Well, the morning of that last mission, we were grounded for three hours by rain and fog that had the ducks walking. I had a bad feeling. We were flying with the Eighth Air Force out of England. We took off with almost three thousand gallons of gas, six thousand pounds of bombs, fully loaded with ammunition and all of our crew and equipment. We used the whole runway.

"Our wing of fifty-four bombers joined up with hundreds of others. We flew upper formation in the number two position at around twenty-eight thousand feet. Because our mission was to bomb the ball bearing factory in Schweinfurt, everybody wore their flak vests. It was one of those days — a day for flak vests, prayers, and good luck charms. Not sure any of them helped much."

"Flak was the name used for the exploding shells fired by the German anti-aircraft guns," Uncle Todd explained to Dylan.

"The Schweinfurt factory made bearings for Hitler's war machines," Frank continued. "His tanks, cannons, planes, you name it. The German Air Force, the Luftwaffe, knew we were coming that day and threw every fighter plane they had at us. Our own fighter planes kept us company partway. We called them our 'little friends.'" Frank paused. "You don't want to hear the rest," he said, his voice almost pleading.

Uncle Todd reached over and squeezed Frank's shoulder. "Only if you don't want to tell us."

Frank bunched his lips and swallowed hard. "What the hell," he said. "We crossed Belgium and had almost reached the German border when our 'little friends' waggled their wings to tell us they were running low on fuel and had to leave us. They had just left when the German Luftwaffe fighters jumped us. I heard the top turret gunner, Sonny, scream, 'Bandits ten o'clock high,' then 'thud, thud, thud, thud.'" Frank pounded his fist against his wheelchair. "Our plane lurched like a big boot had kicked us, then everybody on *Miss Audrey* started protecting their side of the plane. With all of the fifty-caliber machine guns firing, you never heard such noise. Some nights when there's thunder, I can still feel *Miss Audrey* shaking.

"For the next hour they hammered us, attacking from every direction. Parachutes floated everywhere, but we all fought well that day, never backing down. We didn't panic like in the movies. That was Hollywood. We all knew our jobs and we did our jobs well. I'm talking to you today because we did. We looked death in the face and handed the Germans some of their own medicine. There were many enemy pilots that day who died wishing they had left us alone. Everywhere I looked there were flames and exploding planes. I saw bodies and pieces of airplane falling like rain. God, it was bad!" Again Frank quit talking.

"What happened next?" Uncle Todd asked softly, as if taking a confession.

"A twenty-millimeter shell exploded near me and it felt like a baseball bat hitting my leg. Another shell hit the oxygen and messed up some control cables. I thought we had been lucky until another shell came through the upper turret position and exploded. Killed Sonny. Never even knew what hit him. The tail gunner, Mosley, also got hit and bled all over everything. The navigator, Billy, had flak crease his arm — not badly, but it got blood all over his charts. Big Sam took a bullet in his shoulder but he wouldn't quit flying. For forty-five minutes we lived in a madhouse of machine guns and explosions. I was up to my butt in empty shell casings, and we were getting hit hard." Frank paused. "You know, I didn't start out being much of a waist gunner — could barely hit the side of a barn with a stone. But when somebody shoots at you, your aim gets better really fast." He laughed, but the laugh was shallow.

"What happened next?" Uncle Todd asked.

"About five minutes before we dropped our bombs, we took some flak that knocked out one of our engines and blew a hole in the side of our plane. Now we had a new enemy. That high in the air it was minus forty degrees outside, and our plane wasn't pressurized. I felt a sting to my chest and looked down. Something had cut the front of my flight jacket open like a knife. Then I felt wet, like I had peed my pants. When I reached in to feel, my hand came out bloody.

"Didn't know how bad I was hurt because I was too busy firing my machine gun and taking care of everybody else. I do remember it hurt to breathe and my dumb right leg flopped around as I hopped back and forth. I must have been in some kind of shock because I don't remember much pain at the time. Finally we heard the beautiful words 'Bombs away,' and we headed for home. I tried to look down, but the black exploding flak was so thick, you could walk on it. I heard later the bombing run was a success. Parts of that ball bearing factory looked like a moonscape.

"By this time, another engine had been hit. With two engines out, a hole in the side of the plane, and the oxygen supply leaking, we had to leave the formation and descend. We were on our own. Our pilot, Sam, ordered us to jettison the ball turret that weighed half a ton. We needed the plane as light as possible to ever make it home.

"Sam called on the intercom for everybody to check in. That was when he found out that Sonny had cashed in his chips. He also found out that Mosley and Billy had been hit, but for some reason I didn't tell him I had taken flak, too. Maybe it was because he had getting home to worry about. I wasn't bleeding out. I hopped around on my one good leg, and with some help from Max, the other waist gunner, we got Sonny pulled out of his turret. I popped open his seat parachute and covered him up on the floor. He was sure a mess to look at." Frank grimaced as if in pain.

"Are you okay?" Uncle Todd asked.

Frank's eyes had become wet. "The only thing that saved us that day was the weather. With two engines out, we fell behind our formation and we were sitting ducks. We flew through every cloud we could find, cloud hopping all the way back across France, and finally the enemy fighters quit chasing us somewhere over Belgium. It was easy to find our way home that day; we just followed the trail of burning B-17s and fighters lying on the ground.

"We were barely holding altitude across the English Channel, plowing along at two thousand feet. We jettisoned our ammunition and anything else to lighten the load. We all had parachutes, but if we went down in the channel, we would die. The water would freeze us to death in half an hour. Lucky for us, none of us had to hit the silk that day."

Uncle Todd nudged Dylan and whispered, "That means using their parachutes."

Frank kept talking. "By now, Sam had radioed ahead that we had dead and wounded aboard. At the field, they shot up a red flare to tell the ground crews our bomber needed an ambulance. That day, they shot up a mess of other flares, too.

"We came in low over the trees, smoke pouring from the engines. The bump of the landing felt like more flak exploding. *Miss Audrey* rolled to a stop, smoldering. I rushed to help medics get Mosley and Billy out. Then I helped put Sonny in a body bag to remove him. I got to feeling woozy from losing blood myself, but I made sure I was the last one to crawl out that day. Before I got out, I sat down and cried. I didn't want the rest of the crew to see me cry. I was the 'old man' 'cause I was twenty-two years old, and I had to be strong for everyone else. I knew that day I was going to heaven."

"Why was that?" Uncle Todd asked.

" 'Cause I'd just made it back from hell." Frank coughed hard. "That was *Miss Audrey*'s last mission, too. She had more than three hundred bullet holes, two engines had taken direct hits and lost their oil pressure, and half of her tail was blown off. That sweet girl gave us all she had. After that she was salvaged for parts. But to those of us who made it back alive, she will always be the gallant lady that took us to the Promised Land. Home!

"That day we lost sixty bombers and over five hundred men. One of the saddest things I ever saw was the ground crews who stayed until after dark waiting for their crews to come home. The lonely ride back to their barracks when their planes and crews didn't come back, that broke my heart."

"I hope they gave you medals," Dylan blurted.

"I received two air medals of valor and some other tin during the war. But the best souvenir I have from the war is my Purple Heart — and these." Frank lifted his shirt to show a scar running the width of his chest. Then he bent forward and lifted his pant leg to show a twisted knee, distorted from operations. "I got these five hours before joining the Lucky Bastards' Club. Thought I had cheated the devil. Wasn't I lucky!"

Suddenly Frank broke down into tears. As he sobbed, he was trying to hum a tune.

"Frank, are you okay?" Uncle Todd asked.

Frank coughed hard into his fist, then kept humming, forcing out the tune until he finished. Then he looked over at Uncle Todd. "I'm fine," he said, his voice breaking, "That tune is part of the Air Corps' song. The words are 'We live in fame or we go down in flame.'"

Uncle Todd stood and placed a hand on Frank's shoulder. "You're a hero," he said. "A real hero."

Frank looked up, swiping at his wet eyes with the back of his bony hand. "It's all gone now," he said, his voice breaking. "It's all gone, and soon I'll be gone. The whole battle will be forgotten because there aren't battlefields to visit in the sky. No foxholes six miles up. You can't walk up a hill and say, 'Here is where Frank Bower fought.' The only people who looked up and saw the battle that day saw only parachutes, explosions, smoke, and flaming planes. The machine guns, the flashes in the sky, the roaring engines, all of it's gone. It's quiet now. The rain washed the sky clean. People forget." Frank rubbed his eyes again. "I wish I could forget."

Then Frank turned and looked out the window, his eyes staring at another place in the universe, his thoughts as far away as the stars.

Dylan shifted uncomfortably in his chair. He wanted to leave. Uncle Todd stood and squeezed Frank's shoulder. "Take good care of yourself," he whispered.

As Dylan and Uncle Todd left the room, they heard Frank grunt loudly. They turned and found him with his arm raised to wave good-bye. "I was one of the lucky ones," Frank called.

# CHAPTER 6

Because Dylan had no passport, Uncle Todd submitted an express application. While they waited, there were more shots and pills to take. Dylan couldn't avoid the shots, but whenever he could, he spit the pills into the toilet and flushed them. The pills still made him nervous, and when the doctor asked Dylan if he'd been experiencing any side effects, like nausea, vomiting, or diarrhea, he knew he'd made the right choice dumping them. He still had no intention of going to Papua New Guinea. It didn't make sense, going to some jungle on the other side of the planet to look for a bomber that probably didn't exist, searching for dead people who were skeletons by now. Dylan secretly hoped his passport wouldn't arrive on time.

His feelings became confused. Half of the time he hated Uncle Todd. But then there were afternoons when the Corvette was starting to drift at forty miles per hour and he could keep the car under perfect control by playing with the gas pedal or tweaking the steering wheel. At those times he caught his uncle's proud glances.

And he would never admit it, but sometimes he wished he was back with his mom. He still blamed her for sending him out to this place, but her cooking was sure better than Uncle Todd's. And talking to Uncle Todd was like trying to move a brick wall. Reluctantly Dylan admitted to himself that he shouldn't have pushed his mom so much. But it wasn't as if he had killed someone.

———

"We're leaving for PNG on Friday," Uncle Todd announced on a Monday morning after their run. He held up Dylan's blue passport. "And guess what arrived in the mail."

"Great," Dylan mumbled. He scrambled to think. How could he get out of going to this PNG place? Maybe running away would be best. Anything would be better than going with Uncle Todd over to some jungle.

"Have you finished reading Grandpa's journal?" Uncle Todd asked.

Dylan shook his head. He hadn't read a word since getting off the plane.

"You need to finish that before we get over to PNG," he said. "We only have this week to get ready. Once we get into the jungles, there won't be supermarkets or sporting goods stores. We'll be joining the other members of our search team in Port Moresby, the capital of Papua New Guinea, and then going into some of the most remote real estate on the planet. Nothing there is a joke. Be stupid and the place will kill you."

Uncle Todd wasn't one to lie, but with the cannibals and everything, Dylan wondered if he wasn't exaggerating as part of his "scare Dylan straight" rehab program.

He played along, packing everything on the list. But he also stashed away some candy bars and his headphones. A month was too long to go without music.

"Make sure you seal your hiking boots with this oil," Uncle Todd said, handing Dylan a small metal container.

After Uncle Todd left, Dylan tossed the container in the waste basket. He still had no plans on going to this Poopu Guinee place.

Like a clock ticking down on a bomb, each day was one less day Dylan had to get away from his uncle. Each night he lay awake in bed and puzzled over when and how he might escape before going to the airport. Finally, one night after midnight, he slipped out from under the covers and quietly pulled on his clothes. It was now or never. His bedroom was upstairs, like at home, but in the condo there was no porch roof to escape onto. Here he would have to sneak right past Uncle Todd's bedroom.

Carefully he eased open his door and tiptoed down the hallway. As he descended the steps, he froze each time his weight caused a creak. Finally he unlocked the front door and let himself out, leaving the door open. He paused beside the Corvette and glanced inside. It was too bad Uncle Todd hadn't left the keys in the ignition. The old Corvette would be the ultimate getaway car. Who knew what sort of tracking devices his uncle had in the car, though. He'd be better off on foot.

"Going somewhere?" a loud voice sounded.

Dylan spun, discovering Uncle Todd standing in the shadows of the doorway.

"Uh, ah, I c-couldn't sleep," Dylan stammered.

"Must not be getting enough exercise," Uncle Todd commented. "Go get your running shorts on. We'll take a little run."

"That's okay," Dylan said, walking reluctantly back toward the porch. "Maybe I can sleep now."

"Put on your shorts and tennis shoes. I'll meet you back here in two minutes."

"But it's the middle of the night," Dylan protested.

"And now you have only a minute and forty-five seconds. Get moving."

Uncle Todd's voice was absolute, with no allowance for discussion. Fists clenched tightly, Dylan returned through the front door. He turned sideways as he passed his uncle, making sure not to touch him, then he bounded up the steps. He seethed with anger as he changed into his running clothes.

With darkness casting haunting shadows across the street, Dylan and Uncle Todd began their run. "Keep up with me," Uncle Todd said.

Instead of the normal run down to the park and back, Uncle Todd headed down side streets, keeping a blistering pace. When it seemed like they should be returning, they turned instead toward the downtown section of Gresham. The deserted streets and misty rain gave the night an eerie feel. Their muted footsteps sounded like drum beats in the night.

After an hour of running, their pace slowed, but still Uncle Todd ran, not turning back toward home.

Finally Dylan panted, "Are we running all night?"

"We're going to run until you're tired enough to sleep."

Dylan's feet hurt and his legs were cramped by the time they finally returned to the condo. The dim light of dawn had softened the darkness.

"See if you can sleep now," Uncle Todd said, entering the condo. "If you can't, we'll take another run." He walked to his room without looking back.

Dylan limped up the stairs, his teeth clenched so hard his jaw hurt.

———

Uncle Todd never left Dylan's side during the last two days. "You want to join me in the bathroom?" Dylan asked when his uncle followed him into the backyard.

"Just keeping you honest," Uncle Todd said. "Stupid time is over. Now you need to get your head straight and join the team."

The night before they left, Dylan lay awake in the dark, scheming. Without warning, the door to his room opened and Uncle Todd's footsteps approached his bed. Dylan closed his eyes and pretended to be sleeping. The footsteps stopped, followed by a long pause, as if his uncle was thinking. Then Dylan felt the blanket being pulled up and tucked around his shoulders. Uncle Todd whispered, "There's a world waiting for you, son, when you're ready." Then the footsteps retreated from the room.

Dylan rolled over and stared intensely up at the dark ceiling. Outside, cars splashed through the rain in a steady rhythm. Dylan barely heard them. His eyes filled with tears and he rolled over and buried his head in the pillow.

———

Not until they had gone through the security screening and customs in Portland and boarded the jet did Dylan finally admit to himself that he couldn't avoid going on this trip after all. Maybe it would be okay. At least he wouldn't be treated like a child who needed babysitting anymore.

"We'll be flying most of the next two days until we reach Port Moresby in Papua New Guinea," Uncle Todd explained. "Then we'll have two days of travel until we reach the Sepik River on the northeast side of the island. Another day up the river, and then we'll be hiking our butts through swamps and jungles. I hope you're ready for an adventure. One week from now, you'll think you're on a different planet."

Dylan looked over at his uncle in his all-tan hiking outfit and giant floppy brown hat. "We already have an alien being," Dylan mumbled under his breath.

As they settled into their seats, Uncle Todd reached into the side pocket of Dylan's backpack and pulled out the small leather journal. "I want you to finish this before we land in Port Moresby." He tossed it onto Dylan's lap.

Reluctantly, Dylan opened the small journal and began reading where he had left off.

AUGUST 14, 1942

I AM NOT SURE WHICH IS WORSE, BEING BOMBED OR BOMBING SOMEONE ELSE. THIS WEEK WE LOST THREE SOLDIERS WHEN BOMBS HIT JACKSON AIRFIELD. WE ALSO LOST EIGHTEEN CREW MEMBERS WHEN TWO OF OUR B-17s WERE SHOT DOWN, ONE BY JAPANESE ZEROS, THE OTHER BY ANTI-AIRCRAFT FIRE. WE CALL THE ANTI-AIRCRAFT ARTILLERY "ACK-ACK," BECAUSE THAT IS WHAT IT SOUNDS LIKE. GETTING HIT BY ACK-ACK, I NOW KNOW, IS MUCH WORSE THAN HEARING THE SOUND. I HEARD THE DESPERATE CRIES OVER THE RADIO AS BOTH PLANES WENT DOWN. I WILL NOT SOON FORGET THOSE SOUNDS OF DEATH.

I AM LEARNING ONE LESSON VERY WELL: TO KEEP MY EYES OPEN. YOU SELDOM SEE THE ENEMY THAT KILLS YOU. BECAUSE OF THIS WEEK, I HAVE TAKEN A SMALL AMERICAN FLAG AND TUCKED IT IN THE MAP BOX BESIDE MY SEAT. I AM DETERMINED TO LEAVE IT THERE UNTIL I RETURN HOME TO REMIND ME ON EVERY MISSION THAT FREEDOM IS NEVER FREE. I BELIEVE NOW THAT FREEDOM'S WORST ENEMY IS INDIFFERENCE AND APATHY.

MY MISSION HERE IN THIS MOSQUITO-RIDDEN, GODFORSAKEN PLACE IS NOT TO SIMPLY DROP BOMBS BUT TO STOP THE

SPREAD OF TYRANNY. I DID NOT ASK FOR THIS DUTY, BUT I WILL NOT RUN FROM IT, EITHER. SOMEDAY MY CHILDREN AND THEIR CHILDREN WILL BE ABLE TO STAND PROUD WHEN THEY SEE OUR FLAG, AND MAYBE THEY WILL FIND IT IN THEIR HEART TO SAY, "MY DADDY, OR MY GRANDDADDY, FOUGHT TO PROTECT THIS FLAG."

Yawning hard, Dylan turned to the next entry.

AUGUST 19, 1942

THIS PLACE WOULD SEEM TO BE THE MOST BEAUTIFUL PLACE I HAVE EVER SEEN, WITH ITS SCENERY, EXOTIC BIRDS, PLANTS, AND WILDLIFE. BUT I QUESTION IF I WILL LIVE LONG ENOUGH TO ENJOY IT. IF I EVER GO DOWN IN THE JUNGLE, I DOUBT THERE WILL BE ANY SURVIVAL. THE FOLIAGE IS THICKER THAN YOU CAN IMAGINE. IT WOULD TAKE A HEALTHY MAN WITH A MACHETE A DAY TO GO A HUNDRED FEET IF HE LEFT THE BEATEN PATH. THE SWAMPS ARE EVEN WORSE, WITH WAIST-DEEP SLOP, BOGS, SLOUGHS, AND MUCKY TRAILS. THE MOUNTAINS ARE RUGGED PEAKS THAT CAN BE OVER TWO MILES HIGH AND HIDDEN WITH MIST AND RAIN. THEY SAY HERE THE CLOUDS ARE FILLED WITH ROCKS. IF THE ENEMY DOESN'T KILL YOU, THE LAND PROBABLY WILL. AND IF THE LAND DOESN'T KILL YOU, A THUNDERSTORM WILL PROBABLY RIP YOUR WINGS OFF.

I NOW AGREE WITH THIS ASSESSMENT.

By the time they changed planes in Los Angeles for the thirteen-hour flight to Australia, Dylan had read a dozen more entries that spoke of missions to bomb ships at Rabaul and other targets on New Britain, another island that was part of PNG. Dylan turned to his uncle. "All of Grandpa's missions so far were from Jackson Airstrip in Port Moresby out to New Britain. How did he crash way up by the Sepik River where we're going?"

Uncle Todd motioned. "Good question. Keep reading — you'll see."

Grunting his dismay, Dylan kept reading. Several hours later his mind was numb from stories of brutal weather and bad food. Dylan rubbed his tired eyes. They had been flying for almost six hours as he turned to the last two entries.

NOVEMBER 27, 1942

IT'S BEEN A HARD MONTH. I THINK WE'RE BEATING THE JAPANESE, BUT THEY'RE NOT GIVING UP EASILY. I'M HEADING OUT ON A BOMBING MISSION TOMORROW TO WEWAK ON THE NORTH COAST AND THE WEATHER FORECAST IS BAD. I SWEAR THE WEATHER AND TERRAIN KILL AS MANY OF US AS THE JAPANESE DO.

THEY CALL THIS WORLD WAR II. THEY SHOULD CALL IT "THE JUNGLE WAR." IF WE GO DOWN IN THE JUNGLE, OUR ENEMY BECOMES MALARIA, GANGRENE, DENGUE FEVER, BLACKWATER FEVER, DYSENTERY, AND DIARRHEA. DITCH IN THE WATER, AND OUR ENEMY BECOMES SHARKS. ON A NICE DAY,

THE MOUNTAINS MAY LOOK BEAUTIFUL FROM THE DISTANCE, LIKE SPIKES ON THE BACK OF SOME PREHISTORIC DRAGON. BUT CLOUDY DAYS LIKE TODAY, YOU CRASH INTO THEM, AND THEY KILL YOU.

I'M STARTING TO QUESTION WHY I'M HERE. EVERY MISSION, I TAKE OUT THE SMALL AMERICAN FLAG FROM MY MAP BOX TO REMIND ME OF WHY I AM RISKING MY LIFE.

Dylan continued to the last entry — now Uncle Todd could quit bugging him. The handwriting of the last entry was weird and hard to read, scribbled as if written by a child.

TWO DAYS AFTER WE CRASHED

HARD TO THINK. MAY BE MY LAST ENTRY. WEATHER TO THE EAST MADE US FOLLOW COAST NORTH BEFORE HEADING INLAND. ZEROS JUMPED US CROSSING THE MOUNTAINS TO WEWAK. WEATHER HAD US TOO LOW TO PARACHUTE AND THINGS WENT BAD FAST. LAST I REMEMBER, WE CROSSED THE SEPIK RIVER ABEAM CHAMBRI LAKE TO OUR RIGHT, SAME DISTANCE AWAY FROM MT. HAUK AT OUR ELEVEN O'CLOCK.

BELLIED INTO A SWAMP AREA WITH HEAVY TREES. PLANE DIDN'T BURN, BUT WE WRECKED BAD. FIVE OF US LIVED THROUGH THE CRASH, BUT THE FIRST NIGHT, THREE DIED. NOW ONLY GRAYSON, MY TAIL GUNNER, AND I ARE LEFT. WE WILL DIE IF WE STAY WITH THE PLANE. AM NOW BUSHWHACKING TOWARD THE SEPIK RIVER. I HAVE A BROKEN ARM AND AM WRITING THIS WITH MY LEFT HAND. GRAYSON HAS RIBS

HURTING HIM BAD AND IS THROWING UP BLOOD. DON'T KNOW HOW LONG WE'LL LAST.

I FORGOT MY FLAG IN THE MAP BOX. IF ANYBODY READS THIS JOURNAL, KNOW THAT I FOUGHT HARD AND I LOVED MY COUNTRY.

Dylan closed the journal and handed it back to Uncle Todd. "How long did it take Grandpa to make it out of the jungle?"

"Almost two weeks. Natives found your grandfather hiking alone in the swamps, hallucinating and stricken with malaria. He had infected cuts and scratches covering his body, and thorns in his skin, and his body was caked with mud. Looked pretty rough."

"What happened to Grayson?"

"He never made it. Your grandfather tried to bury him, but that was hard in a swamp. Swamp rats probably ate him the first night. But your grandfather was lucky. The villagers who found him were friendly and able to take him through the jungles and turn him over to some Australian soldiers, who carried him to safety."

"If the military read this journal and couldn't find the wreck, what makes you think we can?" Dylan asked.

Uncle Todd nodded his approval. "I like your questions. Back then, this was hostile territory. Because of the Japanese, headhunters, and cannibals, all the military could do at the time was search from the sky, which they did. But that was like looking for a needle in a haystack. With the dense jungle canopy over the top, you couldn't spot a whole army on the ground. When a plane went down, it was swallowed up by the trees and never seen again. The jungle was the perfect cover to hide from enemies, but the worst place for a search crew trying to find you."

"Why didn't the military look again later after the war?" Dylan asked.

Uncle Todd shrugged. "There were thousands of wrecks. The details in this journal were probably forgotten about when your grandfather came home. You can't live in the past, so he probably stored this journal away in the attic along with his other memories of the war. He never talked about his war years. Many veterans won't. But now that I found the journal, we can go in by land and ask local villagers if they know of any wreckages. That is how most of the wreck sites are being found."

"What happens if we find bodies?"

"All that would be left are teeth, some bones, and dog tags, if that. Maybe some watches, glasses, or buttons. If we find any remains, the military will come in with a team to do DNA studies and try to identify them. Those that can't be identified will be buried at Arlington National Cemetery in D.C."

"There's really that many planes still in the jungle?"

"Hundreds, maybe even thousands, are still hidden. Once in a while a new one is discovered. The wrecks are like swamp ghosts. Some villagers believe the planes are cursed by the spirits of the men who died. They believe that real ghosts protect the wrecks." He shrugged. "Who knows — many searchers have gone in and never come back."

"You're just trying to scare me," Dylan challenged. "What's the difference between cannibals and headhunters anyway?"

"Cannibals eat their enemies to steal their spirits. The headhunters, they hang the heads of enemies in their doorways to keep away bad spirits. Some native boys had to prove they had become adults by claiming the head of an enemy. This wasn't really that unusual. Some American soldiers kept the heads and other body parts of Japanese soldiers as trophies, even though the military had strict rules against that."

"That's gross," Dylan mumbled.

Uncle Todd shrugged. "When I traveled in Africa, young Maasai boys proved they had come of age by killing a lion. What's so different with taking the head of some enemy?"

"There's a bunch of heads I'd like to hang up."

Uncle Todd laughed. "I'm probably one of them. We don't do much of anything in our culture to show a boy has come of age. All we do is recognize those that don't grow up."

"How is that?" Dylan asked.

"We put them in juvenile detention centers and call up their uncles."

"Real funny," Dylan said. He stared out the window at the clouds passing lazily under the plane like pillows of white. His head hurt from thinking.

The flight attendants served a hot meal with chicken that tasted like rubber and a salad with dressing that tasted like turpentine. "Why can't they just serve a cheeseburger and fries?" Dylan complained.

"Then you would have to find something else to complain about," Uncle Todd said.

After eating, an announcement came over the intercom asking everybody to pull their window shades down. Tonight there would be little darkness because they were chasing the sun west the whole flight at about 500 miles per hour.

Uncle Todd picked up a book he had been reading and turned to a new page. He had a pair of reading glasses that he wore low on his nose. They had been in the air seven hours now since leaving LA, and Dylan was bored stiff. A movie showed on an overhead screen, but it was some love story. Dylan definitely wasn't feeling love. He didn't like how Uncle Todd always had to have the last word.

"You don't like me, do you?" Dylan blurted.

Uncle Todd glanced up from his reading and shrugged. "I like everybody on the planet. What I don't like is when people do dumb things for dumb reasons."

"So you think I do dumb things for dumb reasons?" Dylan asked.

Uncle Todd took off his reading glasses and studied Dylan. "I'm not sure what motivates you. For example, explain to me why you like wearing your pants halfway down your butt."

"Because I want to," Dylan said.

"So, if you want to do something, that makes it okay?"

"I guess. You wear anything you want," Dylan retorted.

"We already talked about this. I wear what I wear for a reason. To stay warm and because it's comfortable. What's your reason?" When Dylan didn't answer, Uncle Todd added, "I think you do it to thumb your nose at the world. The same as when you say 'whatever.'"

Dylan didn't like where this was going.

"You're bigger than that," Uncle Todd said. "I thought you were your own person."

"I am!" Dylan said, raising his voice.

"Do you deserve respect?" Uncle Todd asked, his eyes intense.

Dylan shrugged.

"Simple question," Uncle Todd repeated. "Do you deserve respect?"

"Yeah," Dylan answered.

"Well, you're never deserving of any more respect in life than you give. I don't see you showing the world much respect. Until you show the world respect, the world won't respect you, and neither will I."

Dylan folded his arms to hide his fists, which were clenched tightly. As usual, he regretted having started an argument with his uncle.

# CHAPTER 9

Dylan hadn't realized a plane could stay in the air so long. Finally he needed to go to the bathroom. The movie had ended, so when he walked to the back of the plane, half the people stared up at him. The other half kept sleeping. The tiny bathroom was a joke, like pooping in a phone booth. It smelled horrible.

When Dylan returned to his seat, Uncle Todd had turned his overhead light off and was fast asleep. Dylan crawled over his legs and settled into his seat by the window. Bored, he pulled out the flight magazine from the seat pocket and paged through it. At the back he found maps showing where the airline flew, with lines to places all over the world. He saw the line from Los Angeles to Sydney, Australia.

Dylan tried to sleep but finally gave up and pulled up his shade to glance out the window. Below was nothing but the Pacific Ocean. They were just one of those lines in the flight magazine. One of the really long ones.

When Uncle Todd woke a couple of hours later, he looked over and found Dylan still awake. "You're going to be a tired puppy if you don't get some sleep," he commented.

"I'm already tired," Dylan answered. "But I can't sleep."

Uncle Todd reached under the seat to his carry-on bag and pulled out a map. He spread it out carefully on his fold-down tray table. "I want to show you how we narrowed down the search area."

Uncle Todd pointed to an inland lake on the map of Papua New Guinea. "This is Chambri Lake, and this is the Sepik River." He pulled out the journal and turned to the last entry. "Okay, so your grandfather first said the weather was bad so he had to follow the coast north from Port Moresby before heading inland." Uncle Todd traced his finger along the shoreline, and then pointed. "He doesn't say how far north, but let's say he went up to somewhere in here. Now let's draw a line between there and Wewak."

Already Uncle Todd had traced a line across the island to Wewak with a pencil.

"So, next the journal says, 'We crossed the Sepik River abeam Chambri Lake to our right.' He says Mount Hauk was about the same distance at his eleven o'clock." Uncle Todd pointed to a red circle he had drawn on the map. "This is the approximate location he would have been if he were flying a course across the island from the north coast, crossing the Sepik River, abeam Chambri Lake and at eleven o'clock from Mount Hauk."

Dylan wanted to say, "Whatever," but bit his tongue. "So, then, what's the big deal? It should be easy finding the bomber," he said.

Uncle Todd studied the map as if it were a puzzle. "It's all jungle and swamp," he said.

As Uncle Todd stared down, Dylan studied his uncle. Why did he want to go halfway around the world looking for a plane wreck? It wasn't like the wreck was filled with gold — then it might have been worth finding.

As much as Dylan hated to admit it, Uncle Todd was right about a few things. Wearing his pants way low was because other boys were doing it, and because it bugged the adults, especially his mom. Using the word "whatever" was a way of verbally flipping someone the finger and getting away with it. It told other people that their opinion was garbage. After his dad died, that's how Dylan felt about any adult's opinion. And like Uncle Todd had said, his headphones did let him tune out the world.

From the moment he'd found out about his dad's death, it seemed like every adult on the planet had an opinion about how Dylan should be handling it. They told him his dad was a hero and that he should be proud of him. They told Dylan he was depressed and he should take medication. They told him he should feel lucky he still had a mom that loved him so much. Eventually Dylan got sick of hearing about everything he should be doing or feeling. Sometimes the world really needed tuning out.

Especially Uncle Todd.

Dylan reclined his seat, trying to sleep, but his mind kept churning with thoughts, his butt hurt from sitting so long, and now two babies started crying in the seat behind them. Dylan would have given anything for his headphones.

He couldn't quit thinking about Uncle Todd. His mom had given up on complaining about the low pants, headphones, or saying "whatever," but Uncle Todd picked apart every little thing he did. Dylan wished that Uncle Todd would just back off. What was *his* weakness? What was the chink in his armor?

Numb with fatigue, Dylan rubbed his dry eyes. They felt like they had gravel smeared in them. He glanced over and found Uncle Todd asleep again, as if he were on the couch back home. He even snored a little.

———

When at last the flight crew announced the final approach into Sydney, Uncle Todd woke and nudged Dylan. "We have a three-hour layover before our flight to Port Moresby," he said. "Maybe we can get us a little bite to eat. You won't be getting many hamburgers and french fries in the jungle."

Dylan shrugged and stared out the window as they landed and taxied to the terminal. Half of this airport stuck out into a big bay like a peninsula, and the control tower looked like something out of a science fiction movie — everything was really modern. Papua New Guinea was only a hundred miles away. It was hard to imagine a place so close could be so different.

Leaving the plane, Dylan followed Uncle Todd through the crowded Sydney airport, stopping to get a burger. There were about a zillion people — families, sportsmen, tourists, and business people — all traveling through an airport Dylan hadn't even heard of a month ago. "I didn't realize Australia was so big," he commented. "I read in the flight magazine that it was just an island."

Uncle Todd chuckled. "A big island. Biggest in the world, almost as big as the lower forty-eight states of the United States, but just a fraction of the people. We'll have to come back to Australia sometime and go into the Outback. That's when you'll see big!"

"Not if I can help it," Dylan mumbled.

———

When they boarded the plane for Port Moresby in Papua New Guinea, it was a much smaller jet and a much shorter flight, mostly over water. Dylan stared out the window at the nothingness underneath. What in the world was he doing this far from home, headed for some jungle?

As they approached land, the mountains down the center of the distant island looked like the back of some green monster — sharp jagged splinters covered with trees. Clouds hung low on the peaks, with mist trailing down the slopes. As they landed, Dylan had an ominous feeling. He was stepping out of a world he recognized into a world he didn't even understand. Instead of seeing a boarding bridge connecting the plane to the terminal, Dylan looked out the window and saw two men pushing metal steps across the tarmac. The minute the door opened, a wall of hot muggy air flooded the plane like a sauna.

Uncle Todd turned and handed Dylan a small nylon pouch with a strong lanyard. "Put your passport, your tickets and anything else valuable from your pockets into this pouch. Wear it around your neck and tuck the pouch inside your pants. Then tighten your belt. When we leave the airport, this place will be a battle zone and thick with pickpockets. They would love to have you wear your pants halfway down. You'd be robbed blind in minutes. Stay close to me. We have a small van picking us up to take us to a hotel where we'll meet the rest of the team and stay overnight. Tomorrow, we all fly on to Wewak."

Dylan ignored the low pants comment. He wished his uncle would take a bath in a shark tank. As they descended the steel steps to the tarmac, Dylan glanced around. The terminal was a big white building. It felt like they had walked into an oven. By the time they reached the door going inside, Dylan was mopping sweat from his forehead.

"Corruption is what makes this place so dangerous," Uncle Todd explained. "People rob you at gunpoint tonight, and tomorrow when you report it at the police station, you might recognize the police officer as one of the men who robbed you the night before. Don't ever go walking by yourself, and keep an eye on everything you own."

The inside of the terminal was large and mostly empty, except for benches scattered around, one small vendor shop, an ATM where you could change currency, a plain check-in counter, and a big mural covering one wall. The bathrooms had old fixtures. Many floor tiles were ripped or missing, exposing the concrete. Worst was the smell. Urine had soaked into the floor and now made the warm air suffocating. Everything looked fifty years old. While they waited with their luggage to go through customs, Uncle Todd went over to the ATM and withdrew some kina, the PNG money. Dylan overheard one passenger explaining to another how the mural told the history of PNG and its people. Right now Dylan couldn't have cared less about the people of PNG. To him they were aliens from outer space.

It took almost an hour to clear customs, and Uncle Todd was right: When they exited the terminal building, a crowd of people hung outside the gate like a pack of wolves watching them with hungry eyes, pushing and shoving to peddle jewelry, sell drugs, even flag down a taxi for them. Anything to make money. Luckily, the hotel had sent a driver, who held a sign up with their name. Even as they followed him to a white van carrying their backpacks, a young boy ran up and tried to grab the lanyard around Dylan's neck. Fortunately Dylan had followed Uncle Todd's suggestion and tucked the pouch inside his pants. He tried to hit the kid, but the wiry boy was already running away.

The driver wagged his finger at Dylan. "Be careful," he said with a strong accent. "This place very dangerous. The rascals steal from you. Do not walk alone. Never walk out at night. Then rascals kill you."

They drove several miles to town in a white minibus, then wound their way through the streets of Port Moresby. Many of the intersections had roundabouts, which the driver treated like a race course. Dylan braced himself, staring in disbelief at the world he had entered. One beach they passed was covered with so much litter it lay vacant. Before leaving the bay, Dylan spotted a small village built on stilts out on the water. All of the nice homes or buildings were surrounded with razor wire like prisons.

By the time they reached the far edge of the city, the neighborhoods had turned into little more than shantytowns with run-down structures and tin-covered homes. The women wore simple handmade skirts and bright blouses; the men, dirty pants and shirts. The heavy smell of garbage hung in the air. In some places, garbage had been stacked for so long that weeds grew up around the piles. In many yards, smoky fires burned, bringing a sharp smell to the air. Almost every backyard had clothes hanging on lines. The hot choking smell of diesel and dust hung heavy, like a cloud. And there was another smell. Sewage.

Low dirt hills surrounded Port Moresby, covered with scrub brush. Even with the van's air conditioner, it was like being in an oven. The driver kept turning and explaining different things, taking his eyes off the road and then swerving whenever he looked forward again. His teeth and lips were red. From the back seat, Dylan could smell the strong body odor of the man — like he hadn't showered since he was born.

"How much farther to the hotel?" Dylan asked.

In reply, the driver swerved into the parking lot of a large pink building surrounded by tall razor fencing. "We are here," he announced.

Uncle Todd pointed at the stained red pavement as they crawled from the van. "That's from the betel nuts that everybody chews and spits. It's why the driver's teeth are red. Bad habit."

"We should have let the Japanese keep this place," Dylan said.

Uncle Todd gave Dylan a withering glance.

———

That night they met with the other members of the team: Allen Jackson, a thin man who had a tan but looked like a professor; Gene Cooper, a big man with a bald head who sweated even when they were sitting in the air-conditioned lobby of the hotel having dinner; and Gene Cooper's son, Quentin, a boy Dylan's age, but taller and skinnier. He wore large plastic-rimmed glasses that made him look nerdy. Definitely someone Dylan would have teased back home if they were classmates.

After introductions, they sat around eating and discussing the upcoming trip. "Did everybody take their malaria pills and get all their shots?" Gene Cooper asked.

Everybody nodded, including Dylan. Uncle Todd turned to Dylan. "I'm the organizer of this trip, but Gene is the military expert on planes. He's also our best medic and resident philosopher. Allen is our survival expert. He's been over here before and knows a lot about PNG and the jungles." Uncle Todd pointed. "Quentin is very analytical, and a walking encyclopedia. He's our go-to man for facts and history."

Dylan kicked the leg of the table. "And what am I?" he whispered. "The group's loser?"

Uncle Todd winked and whispered back, "That's totally up to you. I'm not sure you know who you are yet."

Quentin turned to Dylan. "Hey, did you know that the B-17 has a max speed of 207 miles per hour and a cruise speed of 182 miles per hour? Its range is over 2,000 miles depending on how heavy you load it. It has a service ceiling of over 35,000 feet. Its length is —"

"Quentin, give Dylan a break," Quentin's father, Gene, interrupted. "I'm sure Dylan already knows all that."

"I'll bet he doesn't," Quentin said.

Dylan glared at the skinny boy, but Quentin didn't even notice.

Allen Jackson handed each of them a manila envelope. "I've made a laminated map, a list of the survival gear you'll need if you get lost in the jungle, and a small laminated picture of the B-17 we're looking for. Her name is *Second Ace*. The wreckage probably won't be obvious after this long. She'll be grown over with vegetation. There may or may not be any nose art left to identify her. Carry that picture with you."

Everybody, including Dylan, tucked the picture into their pockets.

"Okay, let's all get a good night's sleep," Allen Jackson announced. "Tomorrow we fly to Wewak and then on to Ambunti. From there we'll be taking a dugout canoe five hours upstream to Swagup, and then we head in on foot. By then you'll all know why people call Papua New Guinea 'the land that time forgot.'"

As they stood from the table, Quentin turned to Dylan. "Did you know that after World War I, New Guinea's eastern half was controlled by Britain and Australia? The island's western half was controlled by the Netherlands — known as Dutch New Guinea. Hollandia was the capital then. But in World War II, because the island of New Guinea was in the center of the Pacific war zone, Japan invaded —"

"Quentin, stop! You're talking Dylan's ears off," Gene interrupted. "You'll have plenty of time to visit during the trip."

"We're not talking," Dylan snapped. "He's showing off!"

Reluctantly, Quentin shrugged, but then turned and blurted, "Did you know that New Guinea is barely a hundred miles away from Australia at the closest point?"

"Yes, I did know that," Dylan answered sharply, taking a deep breath, then adding, "Did you know I can drift a

Corvette at forty miles per hour?" Not waiting for an answer, he followed his uncle from the restaurant. Already the trip was getting long.

Before going to their room, Uncle Todd and Dylan walked outside to the fenced-in entrance to see what the weather was like. Dylan brushed away a mosquito. He remembered the journal Uncle Todd had given him describing PNG as "mosquito-ridden." They had mosquitoes a lot worse than this back in Wisconsin.

An armed guard with a rifle met them. Speaking in broken English, he said, "Do not go outside the fence. Even if you go around the building, I walk with you."

"We were just seeing what the weather was like," Uncle Todd said.

The man laughed. "We only have two weathers here. Hot and raining, or hot and not raining." He held his hand up as if to feel the air. "Now . . . it is hot and not raining." The man with the rifle was still laughing at his wit when Dylan and Uncle Todd returned inside.

Dylan stared in disbelief when they entered their room. It was plain and bare, except for two beds, a table, and some chairs. With a bug screen on the open window and no air conditioner, the room was hot and muggy. Roaches scrambled across the floor when the lights turned on. Dylan undressed and plopped himself on top of the sheets. When Uncle Todd turned off the light, Dylan lay sweating in the dark. "This room is worse than the holding cell at the detention center," he complained.

"This is a presidential palace compared to where we're going. Get used to it," Uncle Todd said. "Welcome to Papua New Guinea."

"Welcome to Timbuktu," Dylan muttered back.

# CHAPTER 8

Any illusion Dylan had of the summer being easy or comfortable disappeared in the next two days. The small jet to Wewak had only about twenty people aboard, with cramped seats. Everything smelled rotted, moldy, or sweaty. Rough air kept the small plane bouncing and lurching all the way across the island. Dylan stared down at the miles and miles of jungle passing under the wings. How could there possibly be this much jungle anywhere on the planet? Suddenly the notion of finding a crashed bomber seemed absolutely ridiculous.

A lady two seats in front of Dylan kept puking her guts out into a barf bag. By the time they landed, Dylan was glad to get on the ground, feeling queasy himself. He looked to see if Quentin was sick, but the thin boy was laughing with his father.

The guard in Port Moresby was right. If the sun wasn't burning like a searing heat lamp in the sky, it rained. And not just a little. When they landed in Wewak, the rain came down hard in sheets, as if an ocean had spilled over. Passengers dashed from the plane to the terminal building holding plastic bags, newspapers, or anything they could over their heads. The hot humid air made it hard for Dylan to tell which had drenched him more: rain or sweat.

If Dylan had thought Port Moresby was remote, it was Disney World compared to Wewak. The terminal was a simple building with an overhang for passengers to stand out of the rain while a tractor and a flat trailer brought them their luggage. Instead of suitcases and backpacks, most of the luggage was carried in gunnysacks, plastic buckets, or any other container that could be used. The search team's backpacks were the fanciest luggage on the flight.

Most passengers picked up their luggage and then stood around waiting for the rain to stop so they could walk the several miles into town. Dylan waited with his group until the rain let up a little, then they hiked with their backpacks across the tarmac to a hangar, where they waited for their next flight.

"We'll be taking a private charter flight to Ambunti," Allen announced.

Dylan imagined a small exclusive Learjet picking them up.

He stared with his mouth open when, after they'd been waiting for almost two hours, a small high-winged Cessna landed. The frail craft looked like it was from an airplane junkyard, if there were such a thing. The faded paint looked like rust. The tires were bald, and the engine coughed and sputtered as it taxied up. The plane swung a sharp circle to stop next to the hangar.

"This was the only plane I could hire today," Allen Jackson explained as the pilot crawled out.

"Well, how are we all today?" asked the British pilot jovially, jumping to the tarmac. Holding his hand up to the downpour, he laughed. "This is just a drizzle. Wait until you see real rain. We should be able to get you to Ambunti today if we're lucky."

"And what if we aren't lucky?" Dylan grumped.

The pilot laughed. "Then welcome to life."

Gene Cooper nodded his agreement and added, "Sometimes you just have to go for it. Life doesn't provide guarantees."

"Now everybody's a philosopher," Dylan said.

Soon they were loaded. The plane's engine cranked over again and again before finally coughing to life. The pilot gunned the motor to keep it going, then taxied out and raced down the runway. Not until they reached the very end did the pilot finally pull back and coax the small overloaded craft into the sky.

Quentin hollered over at Dylan, "Did you know the air cools four degrees for every thousand feet we go up?"

Dylan frowned and yelled back, "That's why if you go to the moon, you freeze your butt off."

"No," Quentin shouted. "On the moon it's because there's no atmosphere. When bombers climb through the atmosphere to 35,000 feet, the actual air temperature is 140 degrees colder than on the ground. Even here it could be 40 degrees below zero."

Dylan tried to ignore Quentin, but that still didn't stop the tall, lanky boy.

"That's why B-17 crews were issued winterized fleece-lined flying suits even here in the hot jungle," Quentin hollered.

Dylan wished he had a coconut to stuff in Quentin's mouth. He would have given a million dollars to have his headphones on to tune Quentin out. They were in his back-pack only feet away in the baggage area, but they might just as well have been on a different planet.

The whole flight to Ambunti followed the Sepik River upstream. The river looked like a brown coiling snake under their wings — a boat would have had to travel three times the distance because of how the river twisted and turned. After barely a half hour, they banked sharply to land at a small, short strip on the edge of the Sepik River. For now, the rain had stopped.

As they taxied up, a rusted Toyota pickup pulled alongside the plane. The driver jumped out and shouted in broken English, "Welcome to Ambunti. Before we go to boat, I take you to market."

Soon they found themselves sitting sideways on planked bench seats in the back of the pickup with no seat belts, bouncing down a rough road beside the mighty Sepik River. On the way, Quentin pointed out every plant, tree, bird, or insect he recognized. He absolutely would not shut up. "Look, there's a yoli myrtle tree. Look, there's a tropical chestnut. Look, it's a rosewood. And there's a pencil pine and a kauri pine."

"Who cares?" Dylan said.

Quentin ignored the comment and pointed again. "Oh, look, there's a banyan tree."

"I knew that," Dylan interrupted forcefully. Wasn't there any way to shut Quentin's mouth? He looked desperately to Uncle Todd, who sat watching the countryside pass by. He caught Dylan's look of desperation and winked with a smile.

Suddenly Quentin changed subjects. "Hey, Dylan, did you know that crew members were issued whistles, and even winter boots with electric heated socks that could be plugged into the bomber's power? They also all got medical kits and gas masks. Some even got forty-five-caliber pistols." When Dylan didn't answer, Quentin changed subjects again. "Did you know that the first aerial bombing took place in 1849 over Venice, Italy, when the Austrian army dropped bombs from a hot air balloon?"

"I already knew that," Dylan said loudly, lying. He would do anything to shut this walking encyclopedia up.

"No, you didn't," Quentin challenged.

Dylan shrugged. "Whatever!" he said.

Uncle Todd glanced over and surprised Dylan with a smile.

Quentin continued. "If you know everything, what's the name of the trail used by the Japanese when they invaded from the north?"

"I don't care about any dumb trail," Dylan snapped. "I don't care if aliens used the trail to invade the planet Earth."

Allen Jackson interrupted the conversation. "Dylan, you need to know this. When the Allies arrived, we were losing the war here. If the Japanese weren't stopped, all of New Guinea and a lot of Australia would have been lost. To win the war, the Japanese had to come from Buna to the north and overrun Port Moresby to the south. But between these two points was the Owen Stanley mountain range, with some of the most rugged terrain on the planet Earth: ragged mountain peaks, raging rivers, cliffs, gorges, and thick jungles. Only one trail connected the two places, the Kokoda trail. But it was a primitive trail with slippery mud and rock. Troops sometimes crawled single file on their hands and knees, clinging to vines to keep from falling to their deaths. If the Japanese hadn't been stopped on the Kokoda trail you might not be sitting here talking as a free person."

"I wouldn't be sitting here talking if Uncle Todd hadn't brought me here," Dylan snapped. Ignoring his uncle's disapproving glance, Dylan turned away and stared at the endless greenery until they pulled to a stop at the marketplace.

For a half hour they explored local wares being sold beside the river. Instead of using stands, things were spread out on the ground on pieces of torn plastic sheets and woven rice bags that had been cut open. Again, Quentin acted like the tour guide. "Those are bilum bags full of betel nuts." He pointed out everything he could see, from dried fish to taro roots, shields and spears, sago starch and sweet potatoes.

Dylan picked up a banana. "This is a ba-na-na," he exclaimed.

Quentin picked up a papaya. "Do you know what this is?" he asked.

"Looks like your head," Dylan quipped.

Quentin ignored him and pointed excitedly at some fierce-looking masks. "Oh, look! Those are spirit masks."

Dylan looked around at all the plants and fruit he didn't recognize. "How do they know these things aren't poisonous?" Instantly he regretted his question.

"It's similar to our country," Quentin said. "All trial and error. With time, people have discovered the hard way what's good and what's bad. And if you —"

"Thank you, Quentin," Dylan said loudly, turning his back and walking away.

Women kept trying to hand Dylan items, repeating the memorized words, "Special price for you! Special price for you!" Several handed out sample slices of papaya and mango. Dylan refused to sample any fruits he didn't recognize. How did he know they weren't poisonous?

As they shopped, a small army of children followed them with curious stares. Most wore only dirty pants. Their little bellies stuck out like brown melons. As they had in Port Moresby, the women in the market wore colorful blouses and skirts. The men wore dusty pants and T-shirts. One had an

LA Lakers shirt. One shirt said BOB MARLEY. Another advertised Tide laundry soap. Dylan guessed the people didn't even know what their shirts said.

Most adults had mouths and teeth stained from chewing the betel nuts. "Why do they chew those things?" Dylan asked, being careful to direct the question to Allen Jackson.

"It's a socially ingrained habit. It's a sign of friendship to give or exchange betel nuts. The habit is an addiction but also part of their culture, the same as smoking, drinking, and drug use in our country. Maybe it's their way of escaping hunger and poverty. Who knows the whole reason?"

"He knows," Dylan whispered, pointing at Quentin. "He knows everything."

Allen smiled. "Let's get on the river. We want to be in the village of Swagup before dark."

———

Dylan stared in disbelief as they loaded their backpacks into a large dugout canoe almost forty feet long. The boat had been hollowed out of a single tree by hand. It had the carving of a crocodile on the front. "I feel like a cave man," Dylan said, settling into his spot for the five-hour ride. Every time someone moved, the dugout tipped dangerously.

Three local men, barefoot and wearing only blue jeans and T-shirts, accompanied them. "This certainly isn't Coast Guard–approved," Quentin's father, Gene, joked. "Riding eight people without life vests in a hollowed-out tree, up a river thick with poisonous snakes and crocodiles."

Dylan allowed a shallow laugh, swallowed hard, and looked into the water. This really was a stupid trip.

Uncle Todd cleared his throat. "From here on in, there are no more credit cards, banks, stores, electricity, nothing," he announced. "We're off the grid. Welcome to Papua New Guinea."

The dugout used a forty horsepower outboard engine on the back to plow through the water. They droned along, meandering past small villages or individual homes built along the high banked shore on poles. Most had thatched roofs and walls made of palm branches lashed together. Twisting smoke rose from many of the huts.

Allen Jackson pointed excitedly to an extra-large structure built high on the shoreline. It towered above the other buildings, with two floors and a thatched roof like some prehistoric church. "That's a Haus Tambaran, or Spirit House. Only men are allowed inside," Allen said. "It's like a church or spiritual place to house the good spirits, but some say they're haunted. Inside, they make elaborate wood carvings like we saw in the market to ward off bad spirits. It's where the men meet and socialize. It is also where the boys live for a month during initiation."

"How are they initiated?" Dylan asked, not sure he wanted to know.

Allen explained. "In this region, with razor blades. The crocodile is worshipped as the water spirit. Ornate rows of gashes are cut into their backs to make them look like crocodiles. They pack the gashes with mud to stop infection. Sometimes the boys die from the cuts. You might see some of these men in Swagup, although up there, villagers are known as the Insect People. Many of their rituals, ceremonies, and carvings center around insects."

"But why do they cut themselves?" Dylan asked.

"It's an initiation into manhood. A symbol of strength and power."

"It's a symbol of being crazy," Dylan said.

"That's what they say about our culture," Gene said.

Dylan noticed that Quentin was sitting quietly for the first time. The skinny know-it-all scratched at mosquito bites on his legs and stared nervously at the water. Dylan chuckled. "This is the wrong place to be if you don't like water," he said. "I'll bet they have piranhas."

"No, they don't," Quentin answered. "But they do have a similar fish with big teeth called a 'bolkata.' They call them that because of where they bite boys when they're swimming." Quentin kept eyeing the muddy river. "I can't swim," he added. "Is there any way to get to Swagup without going by boat?"

Allen shook his head. "This river is the backbone of the area, like an interstate. All commerce, travel, everything is centered on the river. There are no roads here."

"I hear bolkatas are really thick here," Dylan joked, staring at the water nervously himself.

——

The shoreline drifted past as they motored upstream, each curve in the wide river taking them farther into a strange world of thatched huts, women squatting beside the water to wash clothes, and men fishing the shoreline. Naked children swung from trees along the high bank to splash into the river. It puzzled Dylan — why weren't the children afraid of crocodiles or poisonous snakes? Gene was probably just trying to freak him out.

They passed other boats on the river. Some owners had no motors. They used only long, sharp paddles, standing up in their dugouts. Gradually, a steady beating of drums echoed above the outboard's engine. Their driver slowed the big dugout and motored near shore. On the bank, some kind of celebration was taking place. Villagers in costumes gyrated in circles, dancing.

"Sing sing," the driver said, pointing.

Allen explained that in PNG, celebrations were called *sing sings*.

The children nearest the shore turned and stared at the passing visitors as if they were aliens from a different universe. Dylan felt like one. "These people are so backward," he said.

"Or maybe more advanced," Gene Cooper commented.

"What do you mean?" Dylan said.

The big man scratched at his bald head as he talked. "Einstein once said, 'I do not know with what weapons World War III will be fought, but World War IV will be fought with sticks and stones.' If you think of humanity that way, perhaps cave-men were once the most advanced civilization to inhabit the planet. Maybe these people were once advanced millennia ahead of us."

Dylan held back a smart-aleck reply. Behind them, the sun fell low in the sky.

# CHAPTER 9

Swagup was a dirty little village with no electricity or running water. The house they slept in that night was a private home up on poles. A thatched roof covered the structure, but it leaked even when a brief shower fell. For the first time, the mosquitoes swarmed thick. Quentin kept spraying mosquito repellent over his body. Dylan refused. He was tougher than some small bug. Quentin was such a wuss.

The owners served an evening meal of Sepik River catfish, some kind of yam, and funny-tasting rice. They also served thick pancakes of cooked sago starch that tasted gross and crumbled when Dylan tried a bite. Sitting with his back against the palm-bark wall of the hut, Dylan studied the locals. They were nice enough, but because they didn't speak English, they simply sat in the dim glow of a kerosene lamp and stole curious glances. Dylan felt like a sideshow.

At least a dozen other family members slept with them in the large single room that night, some of them snoring. Cooking in the kitchen drifted smoke throughout the hut, helping to keep the mosquitoes away until they went to bed. Like some backwoods hotel, the homeowner had six mats set up for visitors with mosquito nets over the top like tents. By the time they went to bed, Dylan itched all over because of all his mosquito bites. He tried not to scratch them except when nobody was looking. He was glad for the net over his sleeping pad. Maybe tomorrow he would put on a little spray when Quentin wasn't watching.

As Dylan lay awake in the dark, mosquitoes droned around the net, trying to find any small rip or opening. He wondered what other bugs were out there waiting to suck on his blood. Classmates back home would freak if they knew where he was tonight. This was something they couldn't even imagine. Was this what it was like in Darfur in Africa where his father had been killed? The thought haunted Dylan as he lay awake in the dark.

Newborn puppies under the home whimpered each time they wanted to nurse. The floor, made from palm-bark planks, bounced whenever somebody moved in the room. Half the night, Dylan lay wide awake listening to the sharp chorusing of bugs in the jungle. Quentin said they were called cicadas. Dylan didn't care if they were called "fart bugs" — he wished they would shut up.

———

The next morning the team rose early to begin hiking toward the foothills. This, Uncle Todd was convinced, was where they might find the B-17 *Second Ace*. They hired two men from the village to act as guides and to introduce them if they came to other small villages or camps. "Clans in each region are very territorial and don't like strangers trespassing," Allen explained.

It didn't make sense to Dylan. "How can you own the jungle?" he asked.

"In our country, Chief Seattle, a famous Native American leader and speaker, would have asked how anybody could own any part of the Earth," Allen said. "But just because you can't see property lines doesn't mean they're not there. Legal in any society is what you can enforce. Believe me, even with bows and arrows, these people can enforce plenty."

The guides were short wiry men with broad foreheads, big smiles, large wide noses, and black fuzzy hair. Their bare feet looked weathered like shoe leather, but they were agile, walking gingerly with a bit of a hopping motion, each step deliberate and sure. They spoke no English, except for what Allen called "pidgin English." Allen seemed to understand much of what they said, but Dylan could only understand a few of the words, like *humbug man* for *bad person*, *sit haus* for *toilet*, *sing sing* for *celebration*, *nat nat* for *mosquito*, *pis pis* — that one was obvious, and *bolkata* — that was obvious, too.

The trail they followed bordered the jungle to their left and a large swamp area to their right. Within a half hour of walking through the sweltering heat, Dylan was dripping with sweat. Unlike their guides, Dylan found himself tripping and stumbling if he didn't pay close attention.

As they walked, Allen lectured the group. "Make sure you keep the laminated picture of *Second Ace* on you at all times.

After half of a century in this hostile environment, the wreckage could just look like a twisted pile of undergrowth. The picture might be your only way of identifying the bomber. Finding *Second Ace* is like trying to find a needle in a haystack, but we do know she's here somewhere."

Allen paused, and then continued. "Do not, I repeat, do not eat or drink the water from a coconut you have found on the ground. After four or five hours in the sun, it can spoil and make you very sick. If you get a leech on you, do not pull it off. Wait and pour alcohol over its body — that makes it release. If you don't have alcohol, just leave them alone. When they fill up with blood, they just drop off. Always keep your compass with you — there is no other easy way of knowing directions in the jungle. Keep your whistle handy — you can be a hundred feet from the group and not know where you are. Use chlorine tablets in the water you drink. Use sunscreen lotion — the sun is deadly. Drink lots of water — sweating leaves you terribly dehydrated. Always use mosquito spray and keep taking your malaria pills — they do have malaria over here. Believe me, you do not want to get malaria. When you first get it, you're afraid you're going to die. When it gets worse, you're afraid you won't die. This place is beautiful, but it can and will kill you if you don't afford it respect."

*This is just another stupid lecture*, Dylan thought, *like not swimming in the river because there are poisonous snakes and crocodiles.* Lots of kids were swimming in the river. There probably wasn't that much malaria, either. The rules were dumb. It hadn't been hard keeping direction this morning. Even without guides, they just followed the trail. And what was the big deal with the whistle? Anybody could shout and be heard a long ways away.

This morning Dylan had put on some mosquito spray, but despite the spray, he found himself scratching at his old bites. He hated the bugs more than anything. They were everywhere, thousands of them: gnats, crickets, leeches, mosquitoes, and a zillion other little crawly things he had never seen before in his life. It did no good to swat or brush them away. It was like trying to wave smoke away. One time Dylan swatted his arm and killed ten mosquitoes with one slap. He kept spitting out bugs that flew into his mouth.

It was hard to watch where he stepped with so many new things to see. Clouds of waterbirds swarmed overhead. Parrots with green and red wings flashed past in bunches. Huge butterflies of every imaginable color dipped and darted about. Dylan saw several birds with really weird colors and long necks. One bird had a big black body, a white head, and a huge yellow beak. When it took off, its wings thumped loudly, like a chopper taking off.

"That's a hornbill," Quentin announced, pointing. "I was the first one to see it."

"Get a life," Dylan mumbled. Looking up, he noticed a single green parrot. It circled alone, away from the rest. Dylan knew how it felt. It had probably been kicked out of the flock for being different, or for being too green. Or maybe it was just watching the strange white-skinned people wandering through the swamps below. The parrot was probably laughing at them — if a parrot could laugh.

"Look, Dylan!" Quentin exclaimed, pointing at two colorful birds perched in a nearby tree. "Birds of paradise."

"I knew what they were," Dylan lied, flicking a wormlike insect off his arm. A lizard dashed across the trail, vanishing under a rock.

—

All morning they had been walking out in the hot sun. By midday, the swamp felt like a steam bath. Dylan's clothes dripped with sweat and clung to his body as if he had been swimming. Allen kept pointing out poisonous plants or insects. Soon, Dylan was afraid of what he could touch and not touch, where he should step and not step.

In some places the trail passed through swampy meadows of tall *kunai* grass with sharp edges that cut at their arms like little knives. Dylan's boots grew soggy and filled with ooze. With each step, his feet squished. He wished he had taken Uncle Todd's suggestion of coating the boots with oil. Sitting in a cozy dry condo in Oregon, he never really thought he would end up in this weird place. Now, Dylan wanted to stop and dry his feet. "How much farther are we going today?" he complained.

"We have another four hours of hiking to a small village called Balo, where we'll stay tonight," Uncle Todd said. "From there we begin asking locals if they know of any wrecks."

Dylan was thankful when the trail finally angled into the jungle. The intense sun disappeared, but the foliage became dense and thick. This wasn't a jungle where Tarzan could swing from tree to tree. If you left the trail some places, you couldn't crawl on your hands and knees. It was a solid wall of vegetation from the ground up. Ferns and palms grew everywhere in the moist, steamy air. The only way to leave the trail here was with a machete. Decaying moss and rotting foliage left the air ripe and pungent.

Sago palms had thorns that ripped at Dylan's arms, but he had to walk with his arms out in front to protect his face from the twisted vines. They curved everywhere, like the intestines of some huge monster that had swallowed him. Now other new things appeared: frogs as big as his boot, little swift birds that darted here and there catching insects, and plenty of slithering salamanders, lizards, and snakes.

"Be careful," Allen warned. "The more colorful a critter is, the better chance that it's poisonous."

"Look!" Quentin exclaimed, pointing to where a huge fifteen-foot python lay stretched across a fallen log.

"We ain't in Kansas no more, Toto," Dylan mumbled. That had been his father's favorite saying.

# CHAPTER 10

When they finally reached the clearing that exposed the small village of Balo, Dylan was spent. "Where's the Holiday Inn?" he asked.

"Welcome to the municipality of Balo," Allen announced, as if he were the head of the Balo Chamber of Commerce.

"This is going to get old, sleeping in these things," Dylan said, pointing at the dozen small thatched pole huts standing high off the ground.

"Would you rather sleep in the jungle?" Uncle Todd said.

Barking dogs announced their arrival, and quickly villagers peered out from behind trees, huts, and doorways. Smoke from the cooking fires curled upward but hung like a fog around the village in the heavy heat. Under each hut, pigs squealed, chickens clucked, children played, and the women cooked over smoldering fires. The air smelled burnt.

Villagers turned to watch the visitors walking among the huts. Some of the women had no front teeth. They smiled with big toothless grins, their mouths stained red from chewing betel nuts. Some had necklaces made from dogs' teeth.

Dylan's shoulders felt as if they were floating when he removed his backpack. Exhausted, he slumped to the ground. He didn't feel very good. His whole body ached, and he was sweating more than the others. The rest of the group, including Quentin, waited eagerly to be shown around the small village. "You coming along, Dylan?" asked Gene. The big bald-headed man spoke the least of anybody in the group.

Before Dylan could answer, Uncle Todd motioned. "Come along. I want us to stay together."

Reluctantly Dylan struggled to his feet. What could there possibly be to see?

It was obvious the village didn't get many visitors. A cluster of curious children followed behind the group. All were barefoot. Allen pulled out his picture of the B-17 *Second Ace*, and tried to explain to the elders that this plane had crashed near here and that they were looking for it. The two elders spoke excitedly between themselves, motioning and gesturing with their arms, but finally shook their heads. They hadn't seen any plane wreckage.

Allen explained, "They say they haven't seen *Second Ace*, but that may not be true. Sometimes the wreckages have become forbidden places because of the dead. Sometimes local chiefs have performed ceremonies to appease the spirits of the swamps. Once a chief told me he hadn't seen anything but was actually wearing a GI's dog tag for a necklace." Allen shrugged. "We just keep asking. We'll find something."

Because of the jungle, it was hard to tell the sun had gone down, but nightfall came on quickly, leaving them rushing to grab their backpacks. Motioning, an elder led them to their hut for the night. There were no dogs barking under this hut, but Dylan heard pigs squealing, rutting, and grunting. He also heard chickens scratching and clucking, their chicks making peeping squeaks as they scurried about. Under the hut hung the quarters of a pig that had been killed. The smell made Dylan dizzy and sick to his stomach. He fought the urge to throw up.

"You pay for atmosphere," Uncle Todd joked, climbing up into the hut. The ladder was no more than a single log leaned at an angle with notches cut for steps. Carefully Dylan followed. He felt faint.

With no mosquito nettings provided, each of them dug into their backpacks to pull out mosquito tents they had brought along themselves. Dylan struggled to hold the flashlight as he fumbled with the thin netting. He had barely spread it out on the floor when Quentin stood and announced, "Mine's up!"

"You probably practiced that at home," Dylan said sarcastically.

"Actually, I did," Quentin said seriously. "In better light, I can do it in less than two minutes."

When all of their mosquito nets were up, Allen gathered everybody together. "I want you to each look through your survival kits tonight to remind yourself of what's in there.

Here, it may save your life." He rubbed his chin. "Don't go anywhere without your backpack and survival kit. It's your only defense against a jungle that is profoundly beautiful but can easily kill you. From now on, your survival kit should be part of your body."

Obediently, everybody sorted through their kits.

Dylan rummaged through his pack. He pulled out canned ham and eggs, plus bacon, Spam, hash, and stew. There were several dry powders for making milk and orange juice, and some matches — as if he was going to need them in this heat.

The candy bars he had smuggled along had melted all over the bottom of the back pack and onto many of his clothes. Already ants had discovered the chocolate. Dylan grunted with frustration and tried to ignore the mess, stuffing everything back on top. Uncle Todd would love to chew him out for doing something else stupid.

Dylan had thought the food was bad in Swagup, but tonight they ate some kind of rat and more pads of cooked sago starch. It didn't matter because Dylan had lost his appetite. It could have been pizza and he still wouldn't have been hungry. Lying awake in the dark, listening to the monotonous wailing of insects, Dylan felt chilled. Loud, vicious grunts sounded from deep in the jungle. Dylan looked over and could make out Quentin sound asleep under his mosquito net, his breaths deep and regular.

The next morning the group rose early again, this time hiking mostly among the trees. Huge roots poked out of the ground like big tentacles trying to trip them. Branches, vines, palms, and grasses swiped at their faces and arms.

"What was that grunting sound last night?" Dylan asked.

"Those were feral pigs," Quentin said. "They're wild, but they were once tame. Somehow they escaped or got lost, so now they're considered feral. That's what feral means; they were tame to begin with, but now they're wild. If they had always been wild, the —"

"Okay, okay!" Dylan said. "I get it!"

Quentin frowned, his feelings hurt.

A big cobweb snared Dylan's face and arm as he passed. He swiped madly at it, as if at some invisible monster, only to trip on a gnarly root and sprawl headfirst onto the ground. The heavy cloud of mosquitoes swarmed over Dylan like a haze, always biting.

Quentin moved to help him up, but Dylan grunted and waved him away. He stood slowly on his own.

"I don't need your help," he snapped. "And I don't need you explaining everything to me like I'm a kid."

"I'm just trying to be nice," Quentin said.

"No, you're just trying to show off. I get it, Quentin. Everybody gets it. You're the Einstein and I'm the screw-up. Go brag to someone else. I'm not interested."

"I don't think —"

"Yes, you do!" Dylan shouted. He jabbed his finger at Quentin's chest. "You all do. I know Uncle Todd told you all why I'm here. I'm the dumb nephew who got in trouble. I'm the bad kid he has to scare straight with a hike through the jungle. Well if Uncle Todd thought this was going to fix me, he was wrong. This whole trip is a stupid idea."

Dylan stomped off, leaving Quentin behind. For some reason he felt like he was about to cry, and there was no way he'd let Quentin see that.

Because of the thick canopy of trees, nobody noticed the dark, ominous clouds gathering over the jungle. It was mid-afternoon before they broke into a small opening and could look up and see the angry sky churning above them. Allen called a stop. "Everybody take a little break. Let's see what this weather is up to."

Uncle Todd approached Dylan. "Stay close," he ordered quietly.

"You're not my babysitter," Dylan shot back.

"Actually, I am," Uncle Todd replied. "Don't make me sit on you."

Dylan waited until Uncle Todd turned away, and then mouthed, "Whatever!"

He had to go to the bathroom like everybody else, but before walking away from the group to relieve himself, Dylan reached into his backpack and pulled out his headphones. He didn't need his backpack, because he was just going to the bathroom, but he was going to have a few moments of sanity alone.

Dylan walked until the jungle hid the group from his sight, and then put on the headphones and cranked up the volume. The blast of heavy metal music carried him instantly away from where he was. After relieving himself, Dylan deliberately walked farther from the group. They would be mad if they knew what he was doing, but he didn't feel good, and he was angry and tired. He really didn't want to talk to Quentin anymore. Especially not after admitting he was a screw-up.

The trees where Dylan walked were dense, with several small paths branching off. He looked down and could see his footprints clearly in the soft ground. It would be simple to follow the tracks back to the group. He kept walking, each step a deliberate act of defiance against the stupid adults who thought they knew what was best for him. His loud music kept Dylan from hearing the whistles and shouts from the group — already they were trying to locate him.

Dylan decided he didn't care what anybody thought anymore. If the group wanted to play Boy Scouts, that was okay. But he didn't have to. He swayed and bobbed to the beat of his music, walking aimlessly down the twisting trail. He pushed his pants down some. He felt big drops of rain hit his arms but ignored them — every day it rained a little in the jungle. Not until the drops became heavier did Dylan take notice and finally turn around to head back. Suddenly, a sharp clap of thunder sounded over the music in his ears. At the same instant the sky burst open and dumped water, as if a swimming pool had been turned upside down.

At first Dylan walked slowly back toward the group, enjoying the cool drenching relief. Rain wouldn't hurt him. But then he looked down and discovered his prints had disappeared, washed away by a small stream now covering the path. Dylan quickened his pace, but the first intersection he came to looked strange and unfamiliar. He turned and looked back, no longer sure which path had taken him away from the group — he hadn't been paying attention. He pulled off the headphones and began to shout, but his voice was totally washed out by the drenching downpour and the deafening claps of thunder that echoed back and forth across the sky.

Dylan tried to stay calm. He couldn't be very far from the group. Stumbling, he began running down the trail, dodging the branches and tangled vines that hung over the narrow path. The rain stung his eyes. An exposed root tripped him, and he sprawled on the muddy trail. Picking himself up, he rubbed a bruised elbow and kept running. Where was the group?

It had begun with nervousness and then grown into a nagging fear. Now blind panic gripped Dylan. He screamed desperately and kept plunging ahead into the downpour, searching frantically for anything that might look familiar.

How long he ran he couldn't even guess. Soon his lungs burned, and he sucked in hard to catch his breath. The wind and rain continued. The streams down the paths became small rivers, and with each step, Dylan's feet sank deeper and deeper into the water and muck. Still, nothing looked familiar.

Lightning flashed above the thick tree cover like madness in the sky, and the deafening thunder sounded almost constantly. Dylan gasped for air as he kept running. He stumbled wildly through the trees until the path disappeared and he found himself standing deep in the jungle, up to his ankles in water. Then, as suddenly as the rain started, it stopped.

Dylan stood trembling. He screamed again, but for the first time he realized how many other noises there were in the jungle. These weren't the noises he was used to back home: children screaming, doors slamming, lawn mowers running. Here there were weird, scary sounds, strange grunts and rustles in the undergrowth, the screeching and screaming of birds in the canopy overhead, and the ear-piercing chorusing of the insects.

Probably nobody in the world could hear his puny, insignificant voice screaming. For the first time in his life, Dylan felt so very small. His cheeks had dried from the sweat and rain, but now they became wet again with desperate tears.

# CHAPTER 11

At first, Dylan thought this whole thing was just a bad dream. A tiny mistake. A little screw-up. Anytime now, one of the guides would come running down the path calling out his name. They would find him and take him back to the rest of the group — that was their job. Allen Jackson would give him a lecture on survival. Uncle Todd would get mad in his typical drill sergeant way. And everybody would say, "We told you so."

But that wasn't happening. Each long minute that passed, the knot in Dylan's stomach tightened. If only he had just stopped running when the rain first started. Now he could be miles from the group. What should he do? Even as he stood debating, mosquitoes swarmed around his head and arms, biting. Rain and sweat had washed off any repellant he had put on that morning. Walking might help a little, but what if he was walking farther away from the group? While he was standing still, however, the mosquitoes kept chowing down.

Dylan looked around desperately for anything that looked familiar. Where was the big swamp they had walked along? Where was the long log where they had seen the python?

What direction was the village of Balo? Or some other village? Any village! There had to be people somewhere.

This was all Uncle Todd's fault. It was his idea to come on this trip. Who did he think he was, some stupid explorer?

But Dylan knew the truth. He had been a bonehead. If only he had taken his pack when he went to the bathroom — that was what everyone else had done. And it would have been so easy to stay near the group. Allen had warned all of them how dangerous the jungle could be. Already Dylan knew he was a big screw-up, but would this be his last mistake?

To make things worse, Dylan felt the same nausea he had felt earlier, in the village. And his chills had grown worse. Something wasn't right — it had to be almost 100 degrees out. After the rain, the jungle had become a steam bath, so why was he so cold? He shivered as if he were standing naked in a snowstorm. Dylan buttoned up his shirt all the way to the top, but it didn't help.

Again and again Dylan waved at the mosquitoes, but it was wasted motion. Instantly the hungry little vampires returned, attacking his face and neck. Dylan tried pulling the shirt up over his head, but then the blood suckers feasted on his back and stomach. Dylan turned and kept going — he couldn't just stand there. If he walked fast, surely he would come to someone or someplace soon.

Overhead, clouds hid the sun. Dylan realized that even if he could see the sun, he hadn't made a mental note of where it was earlier when they were walking. That was the guides' job — to keep them from getting lost. With blind determination, Dylan plunged deeper into the jungle, searching for anything familiar. But everything looked the same. Overhead, trees formed a solid canopy of jumbled, twisted branches. Now he couldn't even see the sky.

Still Dylan continued walking.

For the first time he really noticed the strange world in which he was lost. Heavy beards of some kind of moss hung from the branches and vines. Flowers with blazing colors and strange shapes blossomed among the deadfall. Everywhere new growth sprouted, green buds, things alive and fresh, shoots and vines beginning life. But there were also decay and rot, things dead or dying. With the heat and moisture, trees probably decayed in weeks. That was the cycle of life. What bothered Dylan was the thought that he might soon be part of the dead-or-dying segment of the cycle.

For Dylan, time disappeared. How long had it been since the rainstorm when he became lost? Two hours? Ten hours? Had he walked one mile or five miles? He existed in a daze, simply here at this moment, chilled and nauseated, mouth as dry as dust and muck up to his shins. He could barely even feel his feet.

When Dylan's chills ended, he began to sweat. He imagined Quentin's voice back in the group. "Why didn't Dylan listen? Why didn't Dylan think? What was dumb Dylan thinking?"

Dylan envied Quentin right now. Himself, he didn't know a single plant or bird. He had no idea what he could touch or eat. Every noise was weird and new. Strange and scary sounds came from the underbrush, sometimes moving away as if scared, but sometimes coming closer — those sounds raised the hair on his neck. Dylan had no choice but to keep going. For the next few hours he trudged down narrow paths, no longer looking for something familiar, no longer waving the mosquitoes away. Just moving.

Finally he had to stop. Dylan touched his cheeks, puffy from all the mosquito bites. His mouth had become chalk-dry but he dared not drink water from the puddles all around him — the murky fluid smelled stagnant and putrid. Dylan tried to swallow, but his tongue was dry and swollen, like a big rock in his mouth. He looked for a coconut tree but couldn't find one. There had been dozens of coconut trees near Balo and Swagup. Allen had said something about them being planted by villagers.

Somehow Dylan knew he had to find fluid. Finally he came across a single coconut tree. Dylan tried to climb the thin tree but gave up — his body could barely stand. Reluctantly he picked a coconut off the ground that looked fresh and examined it. It wasn't like the ones in the market. This one still had a tough husk covering the shell. In any case, it couldn't be too old. Allen Jackson had said something to the group about not drinking from a coconut on the ground, but what choice did he have? Allen was probably talking about coconuts that had fallen a while ago. This one looked fresh — probably just fell off the tree today.

Dylan began ripping at the husk. If only he had his knife from his survival kit. Even after much ripping, most of the husk clung stubbornly to the shell. Finally, Dylan gave up and began striking the husk against a sharp edge of a rock until a small crack appeared in the shell. He held the coconut up and sipped the wet juice leaking from the crack. The coconut water ran down the sides of his cheeks as he drank. When the shell was empty, Dylan picked up another and ripped at the husk again. Once more he gave up and pounded the shell on the rock. It took great effort for the small amount of coconut water he was able to drink. It tasted gross but was wet.

Finally able to swallow again, Dylan looked down. His ripped and muddy shirt hung open, and clinging to his stomach like small sausages were three big leeches, their black bodies stark against his white skin. Dylan freaked, raising his hands up and jumping around in circles. In desperation, he reached down and one by one he ripped them off, throwing them into the jungle like tiny grenades.

Dylan examined his stomach. Each leech had left a welt that now leaked blood from the center. It was at that moment that Dylan remembered Allen Jackson saying, "If you don't have alcohol, simply leave leeches alone. Once they're full of blood, they just fall off. Don't pull them off!"

Dylan wanted to scream. He knew what he should have done, but he had already ripped them off. Why did he always have to do things without thinking? He believed that every-thing and everybody in the world was stupid except him. But maybe that was all a big lie. Everything that had happened at home — stealing, fights, skipping school, breaking into the junkyard — it had all been his fault. And here — thinking mosquito spray was for wimps, wandering away from the group without his survival kit, pulling off the leeches — that had all been his fault, too. He was the stupid one.

Dylan stared down into a smelly pool of water and saw his reflection. He hardly recognized the dirty ghost he saw. He spit angrily at the puddle and kept walking. He had no idea what to do or where to go, but he had to keep moving. That meant he was still alive. Walking made a moving target for the mosquitoes. But walking had become hard. His wet boots rubbed on his heels, causing big blisters that burned with every step and made him limp. His legs felt like rubber posts. His mud-caked boots felt like big anchors on his feet. Dylan had the haunting feeling that if he stopped too long, he would die.

Finally, Dylan stopped again. He could ignore the stinging of his leech wounds and the painful hurt from his blisters, but the itching of mosquito bites made his skin feel like it was on fire. He reached down and cupped handfuls of mud in his hand and smeared them over his face and body to ward off the vicious small insects that kept attacking him. Then he continued limping down the trail.

Sometime later, he glanced up, fearing it would soon be getting dark. And then what? How could he survive a night in the jungle? There were probably animals that came out at night that would like nothing better than to eat a bonehead boy from Wisconsin.

Suddenly, Dylan's stomach began cramping. He stopped and bent over until the big knot relaxed. Then again he walked and again he cramped. This time the pain felt like a knife stabbing him in the belly. The third time he bent over, he couldn't stand again. Falling to his knees, he started throwing up. Again and again, he heaved up the food he had eaten that morning. Then what came up was bile that stung his throat and tasted like battery acid.

Finally, weak and unable to throw up anything more, Dylan stood. Loud growls sounded from his bowels and stomach. Before he could start down the trail, diarrhea began. Almost too late, he pulled his pants down and sprayed the ground. When he thought he was finished, his stomach cramped again. The stabs of pain left him nauseous, sweating, and chilled all at once. Then he gagged up more bile.

For the next hour, Dylan kept moving, taking a few steps and then stopping with diarrhea or more retching. Without toilet paper, he used leaves, which left his bottom more raw with each new bout. One big leaf left a stinging rash. Dylan screamed in anger. Whatever was happening to him was no joke. But being angry didn't help. A swamp didn't care about blame or anger. This was real. The world was trying to kill him.

Once again Dylan hobbled down the trail. The sky had begun to darken with nightfall when he broke out into a small opening where an outcropping of rocks had kept trees from growing, all except for a single brown tree beside the rocks that had twisted upward in a giant spiral. The weird tree looked like a big screw piercing the sky. Dylan walked over to the base and looked up for a few minutes. This would be where he would try to spend the night. But how did one prepare for a night in a jungle? Whatever he did, it had to be quick.

With a survival kit, he could have started a fire. That alone would have been a comfort, driving away the mosquitoes and keeping wild animals at a distance. But that wasn't a choice. Dylan had no idea how to make a fire without matches. He also needed something to protect him from the mosquitoes and someplace for shelter in case it rained again. And he needed food.

The only thing he could think of for shelter was to gather a pile of the bearded moss that hung from the trees. He would have given anything to have Zipper here by his side, cuddling close and growling if anything approached. Why had he ever complained about sleeping overnight in Balo? Tonight he would have loved to smell smoke and hear people snore. It wouldn't bother him to hear pigs snort, dogs bark, and chickens scratch.

Armful after armful, Dylan pulled down the clammy moss and piled it next to the big screw tree. Hopefully the pile would allow him some protection. Feeling the chills coming on again and with darkness fully settled over the jungle,

Dylan pulled off his boots, hung up his socks and crawled under the moss. The pungent wet smell threatened to suffocate him, but still Dylan gathered the musty green vegetation closer to his body to ward off the mosquitoes.

As he lay on the hard ground, nausea swept over his body again like a wave trying to drown him. The shivering returned, and a pounding headache made his head throb. Dylan felt hot and confused. His joints ached and he couldn't sleep. For long hours into the night he suffered through hot flashes, shivers, and sweating. All the while, haunting new sounds echoed from the jungle, vicious and evil. High-pitched screaming, shrieking, and growling. Dylan was totally alone. Never in his life had he craved companionship so much. Even Quentin would have been great. Talking!

While chills and sweats wracked Dylan's body, his teeth chattered until his jaw hurt. Maybe the diarrhea and throwing up were from eating the coconuts, but the chills and fever had to be something worse. Could they possibly be from malaria? If so, Dylan felt like the biggest fool in the world. Why hadn't he taken the malaria pills? They were just little tiny white pills. It would have been no effort to swallow them. In fact, it had taken more effort to remove them from his mouth and throw them away.

During the long night, breathing became painful. Dylan took breaths carefully, as if sucking through a straw, so it wouldn't hurt. Big beads of sweat stung his eyes. Each time the fever disappeared, chills returned and left Dylan exhausted and short-winded.

Finally, too tired to stay awake, he fell into a troubled sleep. His dreams became nightmares. He dreamed that everybody he had ever known in the world was in the bleachers of a gym laughing at him. Then he dreamed rats were fighting over the last bits of his body here in the jungle. That's all he was good for, rat food! Before he woke up, he dreamed he was being eaten by cannibals. At least somebody could say something good about him. He tasted a little like chicken.

# CHAPTER 12

Dylan woke with fire burning his skin. He screamed and rolled over, opening his eyes. Where were the flames? The only light he found came from the dawn breaking dimly over the small clearing in the jungle. Clawing away the moss covering his body, Dylan rolled to his knees and discovered ants, hundreds of them, swarming over his body. The small red insects attacked him like bees. Dylan leaped to his feet. He ripped off every piece of clothing he wore and ran naked away from the moss pile, slapping and brushing at the infernal little monsters.

When he was finally free of ants, Dylan returned to the tree and examined his body. Dozens of tiny welts blistered his skin. He shook his clothes until the last ant fell to the ground, and then pulled on the damp rags. His soggy boots were still coated with muck. Dylan was preparing to pull on a boot when something moved inside. He knocked the boot against a log, and out fell a big scorpion.

"Cripes!" he muttered, examining the insides of both boots more carefully. Then, grunting with pain, he pried a foot into each boot. The idea of walking another day made him want to cry.

By the time he was ready to leave, dawn had brought a warm glow to the sky. At least the mosquitoes and other insects hadn't started swarming yet. Dylan tried to think clearly, but even a simple thought proved difficult. He needed to find food of some kind today. And he needed to find something to drink. If he didn't find food and water, he would die. He didn't want to die. That thought kept repeating in his mind.

Small animal trails angled out of the clearing away from the screw tree. Dylan stood, trying to decide which one to follow. As he weighed his choices, he noticed a single human footprint close to the big tree on the side of a trail where rain had not washed it away. The small barefoot imprint looked to be that of a young child. If there had been a child here, this clearing couldn't be that far from some kind of civilization. Dylan looked around the clearing, trying to guess which trail might have brought that footprint here. He picked what appeared to be the path most used and began walking.

Never in his life had Dylan hurt this much. Nausea churned his stomach, fever and chills swept through his body, blisters pained his feet, his rash from the diarrhea burned, and the leech bites looked puss-filled and swollen. And now the ant bites left little welts that stung.

Still, only one thing really mattered.

Food.

Dylan would have given anything for the canned and powdered food in his survival kit. Now the catfish, sago starch, and cooked rat didn't seem so bad. He stumbled down the trail, searching for anything he could eat. The jungle had plenty of berries and plants and weird fruit-looking things hanging on the trees, but Allen had warned that many were poisonous. And yet, how ironic would it be if searchers found him starved to death, lying beside some plant that he could have eaten. The epitaph on his gravestone would read, "Here rests a boy who was too stupid to live!"

As Dylan plodded down the trail, the dense jungle thinned. By mid-morning he had broken out of the trees into a swamp, but this swamp looked different from the one they hiked past when they were leaving Balo. The sky had clouded over, but not with the angry churning clouds that brought the downpour yesterday. These clouds brought relief from the relentless sun.

Dylan collapsed on a log. His blisters bled and hurt so badly he had no choice but to remove his boots and carry them over his shoulder. Barefoot, he continued. It felt wonderful to take off the soggy anchors that had pained his feet, but now every step had to be careful and deliberate. This was hard in places where his feet sank into the muck up to his shins, or where the water rose above his waist. By mid-afternoon, Dylan still hadn't found anything to eat. His body began to grow weak. He was a car running out of gas.

The swamp was quieter than the jungle, and Dylan tried shouting. His puny voice didn't even echo. It sounded no louder than a cricket across the endless fields of swamp grass. At home, he had always thought he was so important, the center of attention one way or another — usually it was another. But here, he was insignificant, a pebble tossed into a huge ocean. This place didn't care about him. He could die in this jungle and it would be no different than a rat dying. Realizing he was so small terrified him.

Looking around at the swampy marshland, Dylan puzzled. There had to be something to eat. Besides the mosquitoes, there were tons of other insects and bugs. Even as Dylan brushed a grasshopper from his pants leg, other grasshoppers bounced about, thick in the tall grasses. Dylan paused, struggling to recall a vague memory he had of somebody eating chocolate covered ants. Or was it grasshoppers? Ants wouldn't be very filling but grasshoppers might be okay. Hesitantly, Dylan cupped his hand over a grasshopper and crushed it. Before chickening out, he stuffed the springy little bug into his mouth. The legs and shell crunched as he chewed, and a black ink squirted out from its tail. When Dylan wiped his lips, black fluid smeared the back of his hand.

It didn't matter what the grasshopper tasted like, Dylan knew only that he needed to eat more or die. He would find out really quickly if these grasshoppers were poisonous. Dropping to his knees, he crawled through the marsh, grabbing frantically at the bouncing insects and stuffing the unlucky ones into his mouth as fast as he could. They kicked at his tongue as he chewed them.

Dylan captured and ate grasshoppers until his hands and knees bled from crawling around on the spongy, prickly ground. This satisfied his need for food, but where could he find water? He remembered one thing from school; the human body could live for a month without food, but only three days without water. Not having water would kill him, especially dehydrated as he was from sweating and diarrhea.

Thunder sounded overhead and a light breeze picked up. By now Dylan's lips were swollen. When he opened his mouth, his lips cracked. It would have hurt terribly to smile. Besides, today there was nothing to smile about. Even as it began raining again, Dylan had no idea how he could collect the water that fell. He tilted his head back and painfully opened his mouth, but only a few drops hit his tongue. Here he was with thousands of gallons of fresh water dumping from the sky and he could barely capture a single drop. Then an idea struck him.

Dylan pulled off his shirt and spread it out on top of the chest-tall grass, letting the muddy ripped material soak up the rain. In minutes, water dripped from the cloth. Dylan rolled up the wet shirt and held it up so that when he wrung it out, the water drained into his mouth. Brown water squeezed from the muddy shirt, but it worked. Again, Dylan stretched the ragged cloth out, and again he wrung the water into his mouth. Knowing that when the rain stopped, his water supply would end, Dylan kept drinking. Even after he felt full, he gulped and gulped more. Water was the single thing he needed most to stay alive.

As quickly as the light shower started, it ended. For the first time, Dylan knew he had done something smart. For once he had done the right thing, and he felt proud.

For a few brief minutes the mosquitoes had disappeared during the rain, but now they returned, along with swarms of other insects, some big enough to suck serious blood. Dylan kept walking, constantly waving the pests away from his face. He carefully picked each step as he slogged through the rotting and stinking swamp. There had to be a village somewhere.

Some places in the swamp, Dylan had to wade through water up to his chest. He inched forward, eyeing snakes that glided past. One was green, another brown. Two were bright orange. But what else was in the water? Were there water monsters waiting for Dylan's next step? He watched for crocodiles, but were there flesh-eating bolkatas this far from the river? Dylan waded, swishing one hand in front to guard himself. What else was out there that he didn't even know about?

Something big brushed against his leg, big enough to stir the water when it swam away. Dylan fought the urge to go crazy, splashing and convulsing and screaming in sheer panic.

Instead he reached his foot forward hesitantly, consciously breathing slower. His heart beat like a drum in his chest.

Deliberately, Dylan waded into shallower water where the grasses grew.

Though reeds sliced at his arms and legs, he decided this was safer. By late afternoon, blood seeped from long cuts crisscrossing his body. His pants looked like shredded rags. Again Dylan risked wading into deeper water. He spotted more snakes, and angled toward a part of the bog where large stones dotted the surface.

Twenty feet from the stones, Dylan suddenly realized they had eyes. What he had thought were rounded rocks was actually a group of small crocodiles watching him, lying motionless, mostly submerged. Being in the same water with them really freaked Dylan out. It reminded him of the anti-aircraft fire Grandpa mentioned in his journal. When the shells exploded, the puff of black and the exploding bomb fragments were called *flak*. One of the journal entries had said that it was never the flak you saw that killed you — it was the flak you didn't see. Maybe that was how it was with crocodiles and snakes, too.

Holding his breath, a lump clogging his throat, Dylan moved slowly away from the group of beady eyes. He didn't know which was better, wading through smelly black water with snakes and crocodiles, stumbling through the wet marshland with grass reeds cutting him up like knives, or hiking deep in the jungle where nobody could see him twenty feet away? An extra-big green snake that swam past within feet of him made Dylan decide to find higher ground.

As he waded toward distant trees, a dull droning of an aircraft sounded far away. At first, Dylan ignored the faint sound, but slowly it grew louder and louder. Dylan stopped and searched the empty sky, waiting. No aircraft had flown anywhere close since he became lost. Now the droning became a roar. In a blinding flash, a blue and silver plane screamed past overhead, so low and fast that Dylan didn't even have time to wave his arms or shout. As quickly, the droning of the engine faded.

Then it disappeared and silence returned.

Dylan stood all alone in the middle of the grassy swamp looking up, blinking back tears. The plane probably carried tourists from Wewak or Ambunti who were being shown the beautiful swamps and jungles of Papua New Guinea — the same beautiful place where a boy from Wisconsin was lost. The same beautiful place that was slowly killing Dylan Barstow. "Please come back," Dylan cried out, his voice just one more insignificant animal sound in the great expanse of nothingness. He turned and kept wading toward the trees. Down here it wasn't so beautiful.

The setting sun worried Dylan. He had been able to find food and water, but could he survive another night in the jungle? Or was he just postponing his death with everything he now did? Maybe he was going to die anyway in two or three days after a lot of wasted suffering. Maybe it would be better to just lie down here in the swamp and give up — let the snakes, crocodiles, and rats have a free lunch. Who said he only thought of himself!

But then Dylan thought of his grandfather. Uncle Todd had said that Grandpa had survived for two weeks in these jungles — and that was while wounded after crashing in a bomber. The very notion shamed Dylan and filled him with deep respect. He wouldn't have lived even this long if Uncle Todd hadn't made him run to get in shape. If Grandpa had survived for two weeks, Dylan knew he had to make it at least one more day. If he couldn't, he deserved to die. Dylan clenched his teeth. He wasn't ready to die yet.

He struggled to concentrate as random images bombarded his mind: the old waist gunner from the nursing home, the VFW marching past in the parade, the police car waiting for him to quit spinning circles in the junkyard, shoplifting, all the trips to the principal's office, the many fights he had picked, arguing with his mom, drifting Uncle Todd's Corvette. Everything seemed to be part of some big pattern. Dylan's thoughts became clouded and confused as he walked.

Dylan slogged through the swamp toward the trees. He needed to find dry ground where he could spend the night again. Still he watched for snakes and crocodiles. The air reeked of rotting undergrowth. All day he had seen birds, rats, possums, and other animals to eat, but no way to catch them. The only critters Dylan could approach were snakes and crocodiles.

He knew the snakes might be poisonous, and there was no way he was going to try to catch a crocodile, even a small one.

Before leaving the tall grasses, Dylan ate a few more grasshoppers, and then deliberately headed for a root-tangled path entering the jungle. Soon, the thick, matted screen of overhead vines and leaves muted any fading sunlight that made it through the clouds. For the next hour, Dylan stumbled along a trail, no longer looking down to pick his footing. He had to find some kind of refuge before dark, a place where he could be out in the open but on higher ground. He needed a space where he could lie down and still see wild animals approaching. Hopefully a place with fewer insects.

As the light faded, a brief shower of rain fell. Only a few drops penetrated the dense canopy. Suddenly a sharp pain stabbed Dylan's ankle. He glanced down in time to see a dark brown snake recoil and slither across the trail and into the undergrowth. "Ouch," he muttered, crouching. He pulled up his right pant leg to find four small puncture wounds where the snake had sunk its fangs.

Without thinking, Dylan panicked and began running down the trail. But even as he ran, he realized it was probably the dumbest thing he could do after a snake bite. Still he kept running. If he stopped, he would just die here on some muddy overgrown trail in the jungles of Papua New Guinea. By morning, rats would have picked his bones clean. By next week, other critters would have his bones scattered through the forest like twigs and branches. The world would never even know what had happened to Dylan Barstow.

Dylan ran faster. He had to find protection or help.

Overhead the light had faded into darkness. Now the only light came from a hazy moon hanging in the sky like a dim lightbulb. At that very instant, Dylan broke into a clearing similar to the one where he had slept the night before. He walked out away from the darkness of the trees into the moonlight and froze in shock. Ahead were rocks, and next to the rocks stood a tall spiral tree that looked like a big screw. This was the same place he had left early this morning. Without a compass, he had walked all day in a huge circle, only to end up back where he had begun.

Dylan blinked his eyes, as if doing so might make the stupid tree disappear. He shook his head as a wave of despair washed over him, worse than any chill or fever. Dylan screamed, desperate and primal, his voice piercing the hush that had fallen over the clearing. As he finished, tears started down his cheeks, stopping to rest each time he hiccupped with grief. And then a different spasm flooded through his body, and his knees buckled. Dylan collapsed to the ground. The jungle spun in circles. He felt suddenly stiff and cold, as if his body were freezing in a blizzard.

And then there was nothing.

# CHAPTER 13

When Dylan lost consciousness, time disappeared. He remembered little of that night. His body jerked and sweated and shook with chills. His dreams became violent nightmares with terrible ghoulish creatures skulking around his body with toothy snarls and hungry yellow eyes. Other sounds were evil: shrieking, barking, and hissing. When Dylan tried to open his eyes, shadows hunkered over him. He dug his fingers into the soil to try and cling to sanity.

He never knew when night became day. He woke to the feeling of something eating his leg. He jerked and sat up. Nothing made sense. He expected a monster, or maybe a wild pig or rat. Instead he found a small girl wearing only a grass skirt and a T-shirt. She backed away from him when she saw him become conscious. Her curious eyes showed no fear. She was short and stocky, with brown skin, curly hair, skinny legs, and a small potbelly. Her weathered bare feet were rough and worn like leather. Blood smeared her cheeks and lips. Deliriously, Dylan thought of a child eating a big ice-cream cone. An ice-cream cone made of Dylan's blood.

He looked down at his leg and found the skin ripped from the girl biting on his ankle. Blood was everywhere, even in the grass. "Get away from me!" he shouted. "You cannibal!"

She remained crouched, eyeing him. Hesitantly she raised her small hand and pointed at his ankle.

Dylan felt dizzy. "You're crazy!" he challenged again. "That's my foot. You were trying to eat me."

The girl held a bag in her left hand made of bark strips. She edged toward his foot, and Dylan pulled back. "I said, stay away from me!" he shouted.

The girl cocked her head sideways, as if trying to figure out a puzzle. She motioned again at his ankle. "You're talking stupid. You have a snake bite," she said in plain English.

Dylan stared at the young native girl. "You speak English?"

"So do you," she quipped back.

Dylan grimaced. The girl's English sounded nothing like the awkward broken sentences he'd heard other natives use. She pulled a paste from her bag. "This might help," she said, smearing the greenish paste on Dylan's ankle.

It hurt, but Dylan was too weak to argue. Still he didn't trust this girl — her English was too perfect. Where had she come from? "What's your name?" Dylan asked.

"Kanzi," she said. "And what's yours?"

"Dylan."

"Deeeeloooon," she said, playing with his name.

Dylan looked at his ankle and at the mangled skin. "How come you were chewing on my ankle?" he demanded.

"I had to make the skin bleed. A snake with poison bit you."

"I knew that," Dylan said.

"Then why didn't you make the bite bleed?" Her tone of voice was slow and deliberate, as if she were talking to a child.

Even as she spoke, Dylan clenched his teeth and grimaced to ward off the waves of chills that coursed through his body. He examined the small girl skeptically. "Where do you live?"

Kanzi motioned over her shoulder with her chin. "In Maswa — far away." Then she pointed at Dylan. "Where do you live?"

"In Wisconsin — far away, too," Dylan said. "What are you doing here?"

The impish girl lowered her head in shame. "This place and this tree, it's one of my secret places." She looked at him, her brow wrinkled with concern. "You're sick. Why are you here?"

Dylan lay back on the ground. "Because I was stupid and because I walked in circles."

The air had warmed, and the mosquitoes and flies swarmed thick around them. Kanzi reached down and pulled on Dylan's hand. "Get up," she said, motioning to the shade across the clearing. "Don't sit in the sun."

Kanzi held Dylan's elbow as he stood. It took all of his strength to hobble into the shade, where he collapsed again to the ground. The shade felt better, but the insects still attacked him. "I wish we had a fire," he stammered, shivering in spite of the heat.

Kanzi reached into her bag and pulled out a stick, a small block of wood and some dry wood shavings. Her fingers moved swiftly as she bent over and braced the block of wood against her chest and rolled the stick back and forth between her palms.

Dylan grimaced. No way would she start a fire by just twirling a stick back and forth between her palms.

Still Kanzi kept rolling the stick with quick, sharp movements. She stopped once to gather the shavings closer, and then kept working, determination bunching her lips.

"That won't start a fire," Dylan mumbled at almost the same instant that a wisp of smoke curled upward.

Kanzi bent forward and blew gently until a faint glow appeared. Carefully she added more bark shavings and blew again. Soon smoke billowed upward, and in seconds the whole pile of shavings burst into flames.

Dylan watched with amazement as the young girl coaxed the flames higher by adding more shavings. Soon a crackling flame warmed the air. Kanzi gathered damp moss to feed the fire so the smoke would keep insects away. She smiled, then pointed at the smoke and announced, "No more nat nats!"

Dylan felt embarrassed for having doubted the young girl. He wanted to hug her. "No more nat nats!" he allowed. Dylan looked at the girl, so alone but so confident. Who was she really? "My mom would freak if she knew I was out here alone," he said.

A sad look crossed Kanzi's face. "You're very lucky if you have a mother — that must make you happy. I have only parents who are not parents."

"What do you mean?" Dylan asked.

"My parents died in a flood when I was young. In Maswa, relatives take care of children who lose their parents. My grandmother took care of me but she has grown very old. My uncle who takes care of me now is a humbug man and does bad things. That's why I have special places where I go by myself. Everyone else is scared of the special places." She puffed up her chest. "Kanzi isn't scared."

With the fire going, Kanzi reached into her bark bag and pulled out chunks of dried fish and pads of cooked sago starch wrapped in banana leaves. She also had some kind of bird meat that definitely was not chicken. Three days ago, this food would have grossed Dylan out. Now, he ate it eagerly. He had little appetite, but this food meant life.

Kanzi pointed at him. "You're sick — go home."

Dylan shook his head. "I live too far away to go home."

She gave him a puzzled look. "Nobody is ever too far away to go home. The place you said, Wisconsin . . . is it near Ambunti or Wewak?"

Dylan shook his head. "Wisconsin." He spread his arms like an airplane. "I came from the other side of the world."

"Alone?"

"I was with four other people but I walked away from them, and it started raining. Now I'm lost."

Kanzi stared in disbelief. "You don't know where you are right now?"

"Everything looks the same," Dylan argued.

Kanzi shook her head. "No, every place is very different. The jungles and swamps always tell me where I am by how they look." She frowned. "You walked away from friends in a place where you could get lost? Why did you do that? That was stupid."

Dylan frowned at Kanzi. "Why don't you just say what you think?"

"Here in the jungle, many white people die because they're stupid," Kanzi said. She paused. "Stay here so you don't get lost again. I'll bring more food for the little lost white boy."

Dylan didn't argue but he didn't like how she treated him like a child. She was even younger than he was.

It seemed only minutes before Kanzi returned with a possum and some kind of tree rat, both freshly killed. Dylan was too weak and tired to care how she killed them. Hearing her talk and watching the young girl in her grass skirt, moving deliberately about, deft and light on her feet, he remembered an episode of *Star Trek*, that old TV show his mom loved. The crew of the starship *Enterprise* returned in a time warp to Earth and remembered their primitive beginnings when humans still used money and had to earn their livings and pay taxes.

Maybe there was nothing dumb or simple about Kanzi. Maybe she knew more about how to survive in the world than every kid in Dylan's school combined. Maybe the latest clothes he wore from the mall, his smartphone and computer games, maybe those weren't the right measure of how intelligent and educated people were. Around this young, mouthy native girl, he felt really stupid.

Suddenly, Dylan had a thought. It took all his strength, but he reached into his back pocket and removed the laminated picture of the bomber *Second Ace*. "Have you ever seen this?" he asked, handing the picture to Kanzi.

She took the photograph and glanced at it with idle curiosity, but then her eyes grew big and she brought the picture closer to her face as if she were looking at a ghost.

"Have you ever seen that plane?" Dylan asked again.

She looked at Dylan and nodded, her eyes still wide. "It's one of my secret places." She studied Dylan. "Why did you come to my country?"

Dylan felt weak, but he began at the beginning and told everything, even how he was arrested at the junkyard and about not taking his malaria pills.

Kanzi listened carefully and watched him, like a judge preparing a verdict. At first her stare was almost fierce. As Dylan told his story, her gaze softened, becoming concerned.

"Now we want to find *Second Ace* and return the remains of the crew to their families so they can be buried," Dylan concluded.

Kanzi shook her head. "Stay away from *Second Ace*," she said.

"Why?" Dylan asked.

She lowered her voice as if telling Dylan a secret. "It has bad spirits. There are bones," she said. "Many bones."

# CHAPTER 14

Dylan considered his situation as he struggled to think straight. This girl, Kanzi, knew where *Second Ace* was. Physically, he had neared the end of his rope. Kanzi said her village, Maswa, wasn't near. He was still separated from Uncle Todd, Quentin, Gene, and Allen — it was anybody's guess where they were now. So, how could he survive and try to find them?

"How far is your village from here?" Dylan asked.

"You're sick — Maswa is too far for you," she said.

"How far away is the bomber?"

She looked over her shoulder and shrugged. "Not far. For me, only a little ways. For you —" She shrugged again.

"It's too far to go to your village. I can't stay here. You have to take me to the bomber and let me stay there while you find my group."

Kanzi shook her head. "Kanzi doesn't have to do anything!" she said resolutely.

Politely, Dylan asked, "Will you please take me to the bomber and help me find my group?"

"There's bad spirits. Already white people have died trying to find that plane."

"I don't believe in bad spirits," Dylan said.

Kanzi smirked. "There are many things that white people don't believe. And what they do believe makes them fat and sick and weak. They always think they're smart, but when they come to our village, they have to be led around like pet monkeys. They must be told everything: not to stand in the sun, not to eat bad fruit, not to touch snakes. Even a frog knows these things. Many white people won't carry the heavy bags they bring. Do they have broken arms? Are they too weak? They know only their language, not ours. They talk as if we're dumb, and they come here to my country to steal from us. They burn our forests. They dig mines and make our rivers dirty."

"Do they know that you speak English?"

Kanzi shook her head. "No, and they don't ask. I never say anything because I like to hear the stupid things they say when they think we don't understand."

Dylan spoke carefully — he didn't want to make this girl mad. She was his only chance of getting out of here. But she was also being a jerk. "I didn't come to hurt your country," he said. "If you go and find help, where can I stay that's safe?"

Kanzi wrinkled her forehead in thought. "I can find your friends, but we're too far from my village to take you there. You can't stay here alone — it's lucky you didn't die yesterday." Now Kanzi ballooned her cheeks and stuck her bottom lip out in thought. Then, with a simple shrug, she said, "Yes, the big airplane is best. I hope you like bad spirits."

Dylan grimaced. He wished he didn't have to walk — every movement hurt.

Kanzi motioned for him to stand. "Let's go. You need medicine, and staying here doesn't make you stronger."

Painfully, Dylan stood and followed Kanzi away from the clearing. Trying not to stumble as he walked, he watched the odd little girl ahead of him. She was like a graceful cat, not tripping or touching branches, passing like a shadow through the undergrowth. The nimble, barefooted girl hopped from stump to stump, scampering across fallen logs wet with moss, dodging around ferns and vines and undergrowth, and finding trails where Dylan saw none.

Dylan kept falling behind. "What's the hurry?" he called.

Kanzi turned. "The sun and the moon don't wait for Deeeeloooon."

"No, but I need to catch my breath," Dylan complained.

"Does that make the darkness come later?" she asked.

Dylan pushed ahead through a thorny stand of palms, slipping on a muddy log. "This place sucks!" he said.

Kanzi ignored him, continuing down the root-tangled path, moving effortlessly and with confidence. Every few minutes she stopped and waited for Dylan to catch up, her dark hooded eyes showing impatience.

"I'm glad a crocodile isn't chasing us," Dylan commented, breathing hard to catch his breath.

Kanzi shrugged. "It would be okay, because he would catch you first."

"Real funny," Dylan said, gasping for air, his mouth dry as dirt. Hot spells and chills kept sweeping through his body in waves. A blade of tall grass sliced open his left hand like a knife, and the air reeked of the rotting undergrowth. His diarrhea had ended, but the bad rash left him limping.

Suffocating heat rose like steam in the jungle. Kanzi angled to the left of the faint path, hiking out of the trees into waist-deep swamp. "This way is shorter," she said, refusing to slow down.

"Why do you even live in a place like this?"

"Why does a fish live in water? Why does a bird fly in the air? Kanzi lives here!" she said, swinging a hand that purposely splashed Dylan with swamp muck.

When they finally waded up out of the deep black soup, Dylan collapsed beside the trail. "This place sucks!"

Kanzi turned and walked back to where he rested beside the trail. She stared at him with her big curious eyes. "Why are you this way?" she asked.

"What way?" Dylan muttered.

She shrugged. "You're not part of the world. You don't think. You don't listen to the sounds that come to your ears. You don't take time to look at the world. You are never thankful. You don't respect the world. You don't feel when the world touches you, or smile when it's funny. You don't cry when the world is sad. All you do is complain. You think the world was made only for Deeeeloooon."

"Whatever," Dylan grumped. "How much farther do we have to go?"

Kanzi looked down the trail as if calculating, then shrugged. "Maybe we'll get there when we get there." She laughed aloud at her own wit. "Or maybe you think we'll get there before we get there."

"You're not funny," Dylan snapped, struggling to his feet. He kept following Kanzi along the side of a huge swamp.

It was late afternoon before Kanzi pointed to a stand of trees nearby. "There's the airplane that's in your picture."

At first, Dylan saw nothing except dense vegetation. Had Kanzi not pointed, he would have noticed nothing.

But then he spotted the wreckage.

It looked like the huge bomber had tried to land in the marsh, but overshot and collided with the trees. Only the side of the fuselage was visible until they walked closer. One wing had been torn off, but the tail section remained intact. Trees must have been mowed down like grass when the bomber crashed, but now new trees had grown back around the wreck, making it look as if the plane had been set in place with a crane. Two of the engines had ripped off and rested like moss-covered boulders in the marsh grass. From the twisted wreckage, it was hard to believe that anyone had lived through such a crash.

As they approached the wreckage, Kanzi motioned. "Come over here."

Dylan walked around the front of the mangled fuselage. One side of the nose was totally destroyed, but on the other side somebody, probably Kanzi, had rubbed away the dirt. Faintly, but without any question, was painted a large red ace of hearts. Arched over the top, big letters read SECOND ACE. Dylan pulled the laminated photograph from his pocket and stared in stunned silence. This was it. After sixty years, it was like looking at a ghost. "I thought Uncle Todd was just dreaming," he whispered.

# CHAPTER 15

"Come." Kanzi motioned. "I'll show you how to get inside."
She led Dylan around through the tall grass. At one point
they had to crawl on their hands and knees on spongy moss
until they were almost under the tail, where Kanzi had found
a ragged hole big enough to squeeze through. "The edges are
sharp," she warned, pulling herself through the twisted opening. "And don't touch the bones. That is wrong."

Dylan squirmed up through the opening. "I won't touch
the bones 'cause it gives me the creeps," he said, stopping to
let his eyes adjust to the dim light. Every movement had to be
careful because of the ragged metal edges left from the crash.

Kanzi crawled forward in the plane, swinging her small
bag back and forth to knock down the spiderwebs that criss-
crossed the open spaces.

Dylan stared quietly at the inside of the giant bomber. He
could only imagine what it must have been like the day this
mammoth machine went down, the injured crew yelling and
screaming for help, the massive radial engines roaring and then
suddenly going quiet, hissing and steaming in the swamp.
How did his grandfather ever live through this wreck? For

the first time it all became real to Dylan. These were real people, real planes, real crashes, and real war.

As his eyes adjusted to the darkness, Dylan stood upright, mouth open, stunned. There were bones, dozens of them, some chewed on, strewn around as if somebody had tossed them there. Probably rats and other animals had eaten all the flesh. Rodent droppings covered the muddy floor. But there was also a pair of glasses, boots, and a flak helmet with a human skull inside. A ring still hung from one skeleton's hand.

Over the years, storms and winds had washed mud through every opening. But some things looked untouched. Carefully, Dylan worked his way forward in the fuselage, climbing over the ball turret and stopping at the waist gunner's position. The two old fifty-caliber machine guns still rested in their cradles. Except for all the cobwebs, they might still work.

Continuing forward, Dylan crouched as he balanced on the narrow walkway that crossed the bomb bays. Somehow the top of the fuselage had been compressed downward and the top ball turret position had been totally wiped out. Maybe the plane had cartwheeled during the wreck. The cockpit looked like something out of a time warp, with all of its old controls and instruments. Dylan spit on his finger and rubbed one of the gauges. The dust and mud smeared off the glass to show numbers and calibration.

Kanzi refused to follow Dylan forward. She pulled the last of the food she had from her bag. "Come," she called. "I'll show you what you need to know if you're going to stay here tonight."

"Just a second," Dylan answered, searching around the cockpit, looking for the map box. He remembered his grandfather's journal talking about the flag he had stored to remind him why he was fighting. Almost ready to give up, he spotted a square container alongside and to the rear of the left seat. He had to pry at the cover to force it open, but stored in the box, with only a little dust, was a folded American flag.

"Hurry," called Kanzi. "I have to leave to get you help."

Dylan crawled back across the bomb bay, the flag tucked under his arm. Every movement took great effort. "Are you leaving right now?" he asked.

She shrugged. "Is it better if I leave next week?"

"No, I just thought with night —"

Kanzi held her index finger to her lips. "You talk too much for somebody who is foolish," she said.

Dylan collapsed on the floor and leaned against the side of the fuselage, too tired to argue with this smart-alecky young girl who was his only hope of living.

Kanzi squatted beside him. She handed him a big stick. "When rats come in, sit very still until they're close, then use this to kill him. They will make good food until your friends find you."

"You're coming back with them, aren't you?" Dylan asked.

Kanzi ignored his question. "Tell me what your friends look like."

Feeling as if he were going to pass out, Dylan kept pinching his eyes closed as he tried to describe each person. He ended by saying, "The boy that is my age is taller and thinner than me, and is called Quentin. He wears glasses and never quits talking."

"He's like you," Kanzi said. Then she corrected herself. "No, you don't wear glasses."

Before Kanzi left, she brought some big, soft leaves inside and showed them to Dylan. "Use these when you go poo poo. Other leaves can hurt you."

"Now you tell me," Dylan muttered.

"If you go outside, always stay where you can see the plane," she said. "If you're stupid again, Kanzi will let you die. The world doesn't need more foolish people." She turned and gave him a handful of marshmallow-sized betel nuts. "Chewing on these might help your pain, but spit out the juice." She pointed to a place where the twisted aluminum formed a trough halfway down the side of the bomber. "When it rains, good water drips here. Drink all you can. If it doesn't rain, you can drink the blood from rats."

As an afterthought, before crawling out the bottom of the fuselage, Kanzi turned and said, "Crocodiles and snakes don't come in here because of the rats. People don't come in here because there's bad spirits. So what are you, a rat?"

Dylan took one of the betel nuts and threw it at Kanzi but missed. "Looks like you've been here a couple of times, too," he said.

She giggled as she squirmed out the bottom of the fuse-lage. Dylan peeked out through a rip in the metal and saw her disappear like a shadow into the trees. Once more an eerie silence blanketed the bomber.

Dylan examined his new home. Even with the cobwebs, bones, rat droppings, and mud, it was still better than another night in the open jungle. He used his boots to clear a space on the floor between the two waist gunners' positions where he could lie down. This was way better than sleeping out in the open in the clearing beside the twisted tree. At least here he was somewhat protected. The bones gave him the creeps, and the rat smell made him want to throw up. But for the moment he was safe, and now somebody on the planet knew where he was — a small smart-alecky jungle girl who treated him like a child.

After Kanzi left, an overwhelming weariness came over Dylan. He had a sense that he would never leave this place walking. He would be carried out on a stretcher, either dead or alive. All day he fought sweats and chills and had horrible and bizarre hallucinations of falling off cliffs, being eaten very slowly by crocodiles, and running and running to get away from a bad spirit — he could never see the spirit's face. Dylan stared at the twisted metal and closed his eyes. Nothing mattered anymore — he would either live or die now. That was okay.

As dusk turned to night, the sky darkened and became inky black. The swamp awoke with a new sound in the distance, a yapping like wild dogs. Waves of chills came over Dylan, and without thinking, he unfolded the small American flag and pulled it over his chest. As he lay on his back, he stared at the openings in the wreck where faint hints of moonlight leaked in. He felt exhausted, but tonight it didn't matter if he had chills or sweats. It didn't matter if the thorns in his heel hurt, if he was hungry or thirsty, if his rash bled, or if his many insect bites itched or hurt. Nothing mattered anymore because somebody now knew where he was!

Sometime during the night it began to rain. The heavy drops beating on the fuselage sounded like the steady tattoo of a drum. Tossing back and forth in tortured sleep, Dylan imagined the loud hacking of a 50-caliber machine gun firing out the side of the bomber at an attacking fighter. The sound grew louder, and Dylan's nightmare continued. A sergeant woke him up. "Mission's on!" the man yelled, running toward the next barracks. Dylan knew his job. He was a waist gunner on a big B-17 bomber called *Night Rider*.

Today's mission was over Berlin. Almost seven hundred bombers were taking part. Dylan heard the rumble of the engines in the early-morning air, and he smelled the smoky exhaust of the big radial engines starting. He saw crew members praying fearfully. Others threw up behind the tires of their bombers before crawling aboard. They would be at high altitude, so everyone wore heavy flight suits, thick jackets, and pants made from leather lined with wool. Dylan felt the rough lumbering takeoff of the fully loaded bomber. As they approached enemy territory, the bomber climbed to 25,000 feet and Dylan put on his oxygen mask.

In the swamp, the rain beat harder on the outside of *Second Ace*, but what Dylan heard was the beginning of an attack. He heard the rapid firing of machine guns and the nose gunner's voice screaming over the intercom, "Bandits coming in at nine o'clock!"

Dylan rolled back and forth on the dirty floor of the wrecked *Second Ace*, mumbling "No, no, no." In his hallucinations he swung his 50-caliber machine gun around and began firing. His tracers squirted out of the barrel, carving long arching streaks across the sky. An enemy fighter flew directly at him, firing. Dylan fired back. Still the fighter kept coming, its guns blazing, ripping up the bomber. Dylan kept firing, but nothing stopped the fighter.

Lightning and thunder struck over the swamp, but all Dylan heard was explosions. He heard screaming and the vibration of other machine guns firing. Water from the storm leaked into the fuselage of the wrecked *Second Ace*, dripping on Dylan's legs where he was lying. Dylan felt the wet and looked down. An enemy round had exploded near him, leaving his legs numb and wet with blood.

Rats squeaked and squealed, scurrying from the swamp into the fuselage to escape the pouring rain that dripped through the openings, drenching the floor. All Dylan heard was the faint cries for help from other crew members who were also injured, dripping so much blood that the floor glistened. The bombardier yelled, "Bombs away!" and the B-17 banked to head for home.

The rain and lightning let up over the jungle, but Dylan's hallucination continued. With only one of the main gear down and two engines out, the B-17 limped home, then ground-looped on landing, bursting into flames as it slid down the runway. Somehow Dylan crawled from the burning wreck, and then sat in the grass and watched their B-17, *Night Rider*, erupt in flames. All of his friends and fellow crew members tried to escape, but the flames were too hot. All Dylan could do with his injured legs was sit beside the runway and watch his friends burn to death.

Was all of this worth the price? Had they helped to stop Hitler? The questions were like the clouds of smoke billowing out from the plane. They surrounded Dylan, choking his throat and tearing his eyes. He couldn't get his brain around them.

Dylan's nightmare continued in flashes of pain and emotion. An operation to remove his mangled legs. The grim satisfaction of learning to use a wheelchair.

Finally being sent home on the Fourth of July.

The mayor invited him to be in a parade. What a bittersweet honor, being pushed down Main Street in his wheelchair, an American flag draped over his missing legs. At least people would recognize his sacrifice.

Waving to the crowds, Dylan noticed that nobody was cheering or waving back. People were already laughing at the clown that traipsed along behind Dylan, blowing up skinny balloons. Children scrambled along the curbs to gather candy that had been thrown. A group of boys sitting on a brick wall in front of the library shouted and taunted Dylan.

"Hey, you old fossil, find a coffin that fits you!"

"Hey, gimp, why didn't you duck!"

Dylan wanted to run over to the boys and chew them out. He wanted to lecture them on respect, but he didn't even have legs to stand on. He couldn't even scratch his butt.

# CHAPTER 16

As dawn broke, Dylan opened his eyes but couldn't remember where he was or what he was doing. All night, his hallucinations had been so real. Even as he sat up, he looked around, searching for the crew members and all the blood. What was real and what wasn't? He still wasn't sure. Nothing that had happened in the last week seemed real.

His muscles ached and cramped as he struggled to stand. Stumbling around, he stuffed some of the withered leaves Kanzi had given him for toilet paper into his pocket, then worked his way to the back of the fuselage. He squeezed carefully through the jagged opening in the tail. Bending at the waist like an old man, he hobbled away from the bomber to go to the bathroom.

Dylan squatted with his pants down and tried to relieve himself. For the first time, crouched in this awkward position, he had a chance to look around at the landscape outside *Second Ace*. This place was trying to kill him, but it also held a harsh beauty: giant gray clouds hanging like huge bellies from the sky as morning crept over the jungle; the tangled pattern of thick, woody vines overhead; heavy beards of moss and lichen hanging from branches; and the flaming colors and weird shapes of the flowers. Two feet away, a dragonfly landed on a leaf, its translucent wings and brilliant body shimmering in the light.

Thankfully, Dylan's diarrhea had cleared up, but the rash kept making him cry out in pain. The leaves had blood on them after he used them. It took every ounce of his strength to return to the bomber and crawl back inside. To keep conscious, Dylan picked up the American flag that had been his blanket. First he counted the stars again and again. Then he concentrated on folding it, making sure each crease was exact. It probably wasn't very respectful, but now, lying on the hard floor, surrounded by human bones and rat droppings, he used the folded flag as a pillow.

Dylan breathed deeply to stay conscious. Each time he fell asleep, it was harder to wake up. Soon he would simply fade away. Blinking his eyes forcefully, he stared up at the compressed top of the fuselage. What had the crash been like? How much had the crew suffered? The journal said that five crew members had lived through the actual crash, but three died during the first night. Dylan reached out and picked up one of the bones and stared at it hard. It would have been easy to ignore the bones if they were from some animal, but each one came from somebody's father or son. Did those crew members ever think they would end up as rat food in some jungle on the other side of the planet?

Other questions forced their way into Dylan's thoughts.

Had the families of these men, especially the children, ever imagined what their fathers had sacrificed? That they gave their lives so that others could be free? Growing up without fathers, what had the children thought? Did they blame their fathers for leaving home?

As his chills returned, a deep shame came over Dylan. He rolled the bone back and forth in his hands. It had been easy blaming his father for being away, saving somebody else's kids. Dylan realized now that he was wrong. His dad had known that freedom wasn't free. That was why he was reporting on the slaughter and genocide of innocent people in Darfur. It didn't have anything to do with how much he loved his family. Maybe, in a twisted way, it showed his love more. Maybe as he watched those poor people being butchered, it was his own wife and son that he saw. Maybe he couldn't just let their deaths go ignored.

Dylan carefully set the bone back on the floor as big, watery tears flooded his eyes. Why was he so stupid? Why did he have to be half dead, lying in a crashed bomber in the middle of some jungle, to realize this? Now it was probably too late. Even as he cried, Dylan felt himself drifting unconscious again. Try as he might, he couldn't keep the huge wave of numbness from pulling him under.

Once again his hallucinations returned, but this time it wasn't gruesome or terrifying. This time he dreamed a silly children's story of a little rabbit that left home and got lost. He got lost for so long that when he found home, it wasn't home anymore. He had grown so big and changed so much that he wasn't the same rabbit. Nobody even recognized him.

Dylan woke suddenly. A big rat had crawled up on his chest and sat watching him, its nose and whiskers twitching. Convulsing, Dylan swung his arm, sending the rat scurrying away.

Dylan's chills had morphed into profuse sweating. With the sun higher in the sky, the bomber had heated up like an oven. Dylan's sweaty shirt clung to his skin. The last image he remembered from his dream as he woke was the lost rabbit looking in a mirror. The image in the mirror had been his own, Dylan Barstow. What did that mean? Had he also changed? Dylan no longer knew who he was, but deep inside he felt different. Here he had energy and time for only one simple focus: survival.

As he lay flat on his back, his head resting on the folded American flag, Dylan drifted in and out of consciousness. Sweaty heat flashes and chills wracked his body. He could no longer stop the violent shaking. He looked down at his stomach and discovered two big black sausages hanging from the side of his stomach. It took several minutes to comprehend that he was looking at two new leeches. Somewhere in the swamp they had hitched a ride and clung to him, sucking his blood.

He wanted to brush them away but hesitated. In a stupor, Dylan stared at the leeches for a long while. Something deep inside kept him from trying to remove the bloodsucking sausages. Maybe he was too sick. Maybe he was tired of fighting the world. It didn't matter anymore. Nothing mattered anymore. Doing everything his way had almost killed him. Deliberately he turned his head and stared to the side.

Now Dylan felt as if he were swimming through the universe. First he passed too close to the sun and started burning up; then he shivered in the black empty cold of outer space. Next, he entered a black hole, the pressure so great it crushed his skull and vaporized every atom of his body. He became part of the universe, instead of being Dylan Barstow, major screw-up from Wisconsin.

Slowly at first, but then louder and louder, sounds echoed. How weird. There weren't supposed to be any sounds in outer space. Dylan heard shouting and screaming, and then movement, bumping and lifting and being rolled over. Then grunting.

"Hold him steady!"

"Move him slowly down."

"What's his temperature?"

"He's burning up."

"Okay, I have him."

"What's his pulse?"

"We have to move quickly."

"Keep him level!"

"Okay, Dylan, can you hear us? Dylan, wake up. Can you hear me?"

Dylan felt rain on his face but that wasn't right — there wasn't rain in outer space, and surely not in a black hole. Something pried his eyes open and held his head up to put fluid in his mouth. He coughed and choked on the fluid. Now his clothes were being removed. But if he was in space, that would be his space suit. Taking his space suit off would kill him, so Dylan tried to swing his arms and fight back. He couldn't let anybody take his space suit off.

Strong hands held him still. Something was being pried from his fingers. He couldn't fight against all the hands that gripped him. Why were they trying to kill him? What were they doing taking off his space suit? Then more voices sounded.

"Make sure his airway is clear."

"Hold his arm. We have to get some medication onboard for his malaria."

"How could he have gotten malaria?"

"Keep giving him fluids — he's dehydrated."

"Looks like a snake bit his ankle."

"What ripped the skin up so bad?"

"Looks like the jungle tried to kill him."

"Okay, somebody cover him with bug spray and suntan lotion — we need to get moving."

Then Dylan felt jostling motion. He wanted everything to be still again. He wanted to float again through space. Instead it was as if he were being dragged down a bumpy dirt road. He felt powerless, and every movement hurt. He tried to shout, but a huge hand pinched his throat. Another strong hand kept him from sitting up. He tried to open his eyes but they felt glued closed. Finally Dylan gave up and clenched his teeth to ward off the pounding pain. If this was what it felt like to die, he wanted to get it over with. But the end refused to come.

———

It seemed forever before the bumping and jostling finally subsided into stillness. Dylan lay unconscious in a pole house in Balo, never seeing the villagers' eyes peeking in at him during his heavy slumber. Ghostly voices whispered in the distance — different voices than those that whispered across the room.

Dylan woke once during the night, long enough to wonder where he was and what had happened. A slight breeze blew through the palm planks covering the walls.

Not until morning could he finally open his eyes and stare up at a ring of concerned faces: Uncle Todd, Quentin, Allen Jackson, Gene Cooper, a young, tired-looking woman from the village, and an odd old man. They all stood looking down at him. Dylan eyed the old man. His skin was wrinkled as a prune. His whole body had been rubbed with coals from a fire, making him all black except for his face, which was painted white. Painted with the shapes of a skull. A necklace of shells, dogs' teeth, and feathers hung from his neck. Bones hung from his stretched earlobes. Only a breechcloth of leaves covered his lower body, like a skirt, swishing each time he moved. Dylan stared at the strange man.

"Hey, how are you doing, trooper?" Uncle Todd asked, reaching down and placing the folded American flag on Dylan's chest. "We found you hugging this in the bomber."

Dylan ran his hand over the soft cloth. "Thanks," he said, his voice scratchy. "That was the flag Grandpa talked about in his journal."

"Hey, Dylan. We were worried about you," Quentin said.

Dylan wanted to close his eyes to escape the stares. "I screwed up," he mumbled.

"How you feeling?" Allen asked.

"Like a truck hit me," Dylan said.

The old man with the painted black body smiled at Dylan. "I must leave now," he said. He stooped and touched Dylan's forehead gently, then he walked to the ladder and began crawling down. Before his head disappeared, he called, "Good-bye, Deeeeloooon."

Dylan jerked his head up to look, but the man had disappeared. "Who was that guy? A witch doctor?" he blurted.

"He saved your life," Uncle Todd said. "He came and told our group where you were. Told us how he helped you find the bomber. Not sure we would have believed him except he knew the name *Second Ace* and he described you and the clothes you wore."

"I didn't meet that old man," Dylan said. "I've never seen him before."

Uncle Todd shook his head. "You must have. Maybe you were delirious. He said his name was Kanzi."

Dylan stared, wide-eyed, and shook his head. "No, no, no," he stammered. "Kanzi was a young girl, younger than me. She said she was from a village called Maswa."

Uncle Todd shook his head. "Kanzi was definitely that old man. He said he started a fire for you, fed you, and led you to *Second Ace.*"

The young village woman put her hand on Uncle Todd's arm. She spoke quietly, with broken English. "No village called Maswa. *Maswa* means *dreams*. Kanzi, he be who he needs to be."

"What do you mean?" Gene Cooper asked.

"Many people come here for bad reason. Some look for airplanes to steal engines or take money from dead people. Kanzi sometimes kills people with bad reasons. Kanzi knows you come for good reasons. That is why he lets you live." She looked at Dylan. "Kanzi knows you have good heart."

Dylan shook his head. "I wasn't crazy. Kanzi was just a young girl. She bit on my ankle and made it bleed because of the snake poison. She started a fire and brought me food. I know she was real."

The young woman nodded, toying with the reed bag she carried. "Kanzi is a girl for you because you need a girl to help you."

Dylan bit his tongue — he didn't need any girl to help him! But even as the thought came to him, he knew he had needed Kanzi desperately. Maybe someone younger, with an innocent face and a sharp tongue to make him feel humble. That was exactly what he had needed.

The bashful woman turned to Gene Cooper. "You needed old man painted with black to help you believe." She raised her hands upward. "Maybe everything is real. Maybe nothing is real. Real is what we believe. We all believe different. I think today Kanzi comes to say good-bye to all of you."

Gene Cooper turned and stared at the pole ladder Kanzi had climbed down, then he turned back and spoke to Dylan. "Right now, you need a hospital. You were in rough shape last evening when we found you inside *Second Ace*, so we brought you here to Balo. If you're up for it, we'll carry you to Swagup today. Then we have a dugout canoe ready to take us back to Ambunti."

Uncle Todd stood nearby, unable to hide his worry and stress. When he spoke, his voice sounded angry. "If you're still alive, a plane will take you to Port Moresby, where we'll get you into a hospital until you can travel back to the US. We're not going to rush things. You've been through a lot."

Dylan looked up. "Thanks, everybody, for helping me," he said.

"While we get ready, you get more sleep," Gene said, motioning for the rest to leave.

Dylan panicked. "Somebody stay here," he pleaded.

"I'll stay," Quentin said.

"Is that okay?" Gene asked.

Dylan nodded. "I don't want to be alone."

As everybody left, Quentin sat down beside Dylan's pad on the hard floor. He adjusted the mosquito netting. "Man, we looked all over for you," he said. When Dylan didn't answer, Quentin kept talking. "Our guides had three villages searching. It was like you disappeared into nowhere. One second you were there, the next second you evaporated. I thought you had died or maybe some critter had gotten you. I was thinking that if you had —" Suddenly Quentin stopped. "I shouldn't be talking so much, should I? You need to sleep."

Dylan reached his hand toward Quentin until it touched the netting. "I don't ever want to be alone again in my life. Please keep talking," he said.

# CHAPTER 17

When Dylan woke next, he was being lowered down the notched pole ladder, the same ladder the old man who had claimed to be Kanzi had crawled down. Dylan's body ached, and he felt drained of all energy. Carefully, Uncle Todd and Allen placed him on a rough stretcher they had fashioned from two poles and some canvas. Two men from the village had been hired to guide them and to help carry Dylan through the jungle and swamp to Swagup.

As they left, Dylan clenched his teeth against the constant jarring. It had rained most of the night, and each time one of the carriers brushed against a bush or a tree, a shower of water drenched the stretcher. Everybody took turns helping to carry Dylan, even Quentin. In the suffocating heat, sometimes they traded turns every hundred yards.

Dylan tried to take his mind off the jarring pain by looking up at the steaming jungle. He smelled the trees, the palms, the mosses, and the heavy, pungent odor of decay. For the first time, he noticed how the smells were stronger after rain. And he heard sounds in a way he had never noticed, the rustling in the underbrush, wind blowing through the jungle canopy, and birds and insects chorusing with a piercing harmony. The sounds were beautiful.

Suddenly, Dylan felt sick to his stomach and he turned sideways and threw up. He had never felt so rough in his life. Allen had put alcohol on the leeches to remove them, but the hot and cold flashes persisted. Dylan's insect bites and sunburn covered his body with boils and welts. The thorns in his heels had infected and oozed pus. His arms ached from gripping the stretcher poles. Worst was his ankle, which was still swollen from the snake bite. He could no longer put weight on that foot. Even lying on the stretcher, it ached.

Struggling to carry Dylan across a deep stretch of swamp, Allen Jackson lost his balance. Dylan found himself suddenly swimming to keep his head up. Uncle Todd helped Dylan back onto the stretcher. "Hang in there," he said, his words sounding more like a command than encouragement.

When Quentin took his next turn carrying the stretcher, he asked Dylan, "Why did you walk away from everybody?"

Dylan didn't want to think. "I was mad," he mumbled.

"Because of me?"

"No. Because of a lot of things, most of which had nothing to do with you. I didn't want to be here anymore."

Quentin breathed heavily. "Lots of times I don't get what I want, but I don't walk away into a jungle," he said.

"I was just being stupid," Dylan admitted.

Quentin was quiet for a moment. "Well, you found *Second Ace*," he said finally. "And you survived. I don't know what I would have done if I'd gotten lost. Freaked, probably. But you aren't a screw-up. At least I don't think so."

"Thanks," Dylan said, his voice shaking. He closed his eyes tightly. He felt hot and wet. "That means a lot, Quentin."

—

To keep Dylan from falling off, Uncle Todd and Gene Cooper wrapped a rope around the stretcher, tying Dylan to it. Each time the team traded turns carrying him, they took a short rest. During one rest, Dylan asked in a coarse whisper, "Did you guys get what you needed at the bomber?"

Gene shrugged. "We couldn't spend as much time at the wreckage as we would have liked, because we had to get you out of there. We were able to establish coordinates for finding it again. Quentin found two sets of dog tags, and we took a number of pictures that will help with recovery."

"What happens now?" Dylan asked.

"You get rest," Gene suggested.

"I won't rest until I get off this stretcher," Dylan said. "What happens now with *Second Ace*?"

"A U.S. Marines recovery team will come in. That team will be made up of forensic anthropologists, a communications officer, explosive disposal officers in case there are live bombs, and a whole slew of other experts."

"What happens to the bones?" Dylan asked.

"Everything they find will be taken to Hawaii for identification. Individual remains will be returned to their families. A separate memorial service will be held at the Tomb of the

Unknown Soldier in Arlington National Cemetery out in D.C. for the remains that can't be identified. That ceremony will honor and recognize the whole crew."

"It's too bad this didn't happen years ago," Dylan remarked. "Grandpa could have been there."

"It's hard finding wrecks in the jungle," Gene said. "The PNG government doesn't want them removed, saying they're a part of their country's history and could bring tourist money to the region. Local chieftains often think they're sacred because of the dead. For some crew members, the memories are too hard. And —" He shrugged. "Some people just don't care anymore." He looked at Dylan, who was still clutching the folded American flag. "Do you want me to put that flag in my backpack?"

"No," Dylan replied. "I'm going to be the one who takes it home. It belonged to Grandpa."

"What are you going to do with it?" Gene asked.

"Haven't decided yet," Dylan said.

"Whatever you do, I'm sure it would have made your grandfather proud."

Dylan grew silent. He hadn't made anybody proud with anything he had done. "There's so much stuff I didn't know," he said.

Gene gave him a curious look, allowed a guarded smile, and then nodded. "Okay, everybody, let's hit the trail again. Swagup isn't getting any closer."

By the time they reached Swagup, the setting sun cast long shadows. Everybody had reached the end of their endurance. Even holding the flag was now a struggle for Dylan. When they helped him from the stretcher, his leg gave out and he fell hard to the ground. His swollen ankle had doubled in size and pained him terribly. Huge beads of sweat dripped from Dylan's face, and his body burned with fever.

"You're in a bad way!" Gene exclaimed. "Let's get you lying down where I can check you over."

"I'll help," Quentin volunteered. He and his father helped Dylan up and carried him to the pole hut where they would all sleep that night. It took everybody to lift Dylan up the steep ladder to the main floor. Carefully Gene took Dylan's blood pressure and temperature, then examined every inch of his body.

Dylan rested, listening to everyone talk, Hearing voices again was sweet music. There were times in the jungle when he had thought he would never again hear another human voice. For a short time, Dylan passed out. When he awoke, he found the team gathered in one corner of the small hut, whispering to each other.

Dylan called out, "Hey, what's the big secret?"

"It's nothing," Allen said, turning. "Just planning tomorrow."

Dylan watched the family who owned the pole hut as they prepared the evening meal. He realized how kind and giving the villages of Papua New Guinea could be. He had come over here afraid of cannibals and headhunters, thinking everybody was backward and uncivilized. What he had found was kindness. They didn't have to help a stupid teenager from America. His life meant nothing to them. But again and again complete strangers had helped their team. During the last week, Dylan had come to feel that he was the one who was uncivilized. He was the one whose world was all screwed up.

Quentin interrupted Dylan's thoughts, bringing food. "Here, eat something," he pleaded. "You need to do everything you can to help your body recover."

"I'm already better," Dylan said.

"No you're not!" Quentin said forcefully, as if he knew something that Dylan didn't.

Reluctantly, Dylan forced down some cooked sago and salted fish. The rain water he drank in the jungle was better than the water here. This stuff had iodine from pills Allen Jackson added to kill germs and bacteria.

Villagers kept crawling up the ladder to peek at the white boy who almost died in the jungle — the one who had met Kanzi. By bedtime, Dylan felt really rough. The infection in his leg had grown worse. It hurt to even touch his ankle.

Before going to sleep, the team gathered around Dylan. He could tell from their faces that serious news was coming.

"Dylan, I'm sorry to have to tell you this, but you have bad gangrene in your leg," Gene said bluntly. "That means your cells are dying, and bacteria have begun to grow in the tissue. The hospital may have to amputate, or it could kill you."

"You mean cut my leg off?" Dylan exclaimed.

Gene nodded. "It all depends on how fast we can get you to Australia. Sydney will be your best chance now. Not Port Moresby."

"That's what you guys were whispering about," Dylan said.

Uncle Todd nodded, his expression grim.

Dylan's chest felt suddenly tight. The small hut seemed to press inward. He couldn't believe this. His eyes grew hot, and it took all his strength to hold back his tears. "This wouldn't have happened if Mom hadn't sent me to your place. It's all her fault!" he blurted.

Uncle Todd spoke sharply. "Don't you dare blame your mom or me or anyone else for what happened. You will never know how hard it was for your mother to call me for help. You're the one who pulled this dumb stunt in the jungle that almost killed you."

Dylan felt a sudden shame. This was the first time he had seen his uncle show real anger. He knew Uncle Todd was right, but he had wanted desperately to blame someone else. Being mad had always been easier than looking in the mirror. "I'm sorry," he said. "I didn't mean it that way."

Uncle Todd hesitated as if wanting to say something. Then he turned to leave. "We leave early to take a dugout down the Sepik to Ambunti. Get some sleep — you'll need it. Hopefully we can fly you direct from Ambunti to Port Moresby instead of going through Wewak. Your leg may depend on it."

Quentin remained beside Dylan's mosquito netting after the rest left. When the gas lantern was turned off, Quentin sat down on the floor. "Are you mad at me?" he whispered in the dark.

"No," Dylan whispered back. "What makes you think that?"

"I don't have any friends back home. Dad tells me I talk too much, and that I always act like I know everything. It's not like I know everything, but I do know a lot of stuff. Once a guy stopped me in a store and —"

"Your talking didn't give me gangrene in my leg," Dylan interrupted. "Not yet."

"A person couldn't get gangrene in their leg from talking unless you sat on that leg. Maybe then the leg could lose circulation and —"

"I was just joking," Dylan said. "Go get some sleep."

Quentin allowed a shallow laugh. "Uh, oh yeah, you were just joking." He stood and paused awkwardly in the dark. "I really hope you don't lose your leg."

"Thanks. I'll be okay." As Quentin turned to leave, Dylan whispered, "You helped save my life. Nobody would do that except a friend."

Dylan thought he heard a sniffle in the dark. "That's cool," Quentin said, disappearing into the darkness with a small flashlight he had turned on.

Dylan reached down and felt his ankle. It was hot, swollen, and numb as a post. He had a sick feeling inside as he stared up into the darkness. Already somebody snored loudly.

Dylan slept little all night, tossing back and forth, grimacing. Each time he rolled over, his ankle made him cry out with pain. Between the nausea, pain, fever, and chills, the dark night became a living hell.

When the team rose before daylight, Dylan felt numb with exhaustion. Once again he was lowered down the ladder and carried the short distance to the shore of the Sepik River. Gene insisted that he eat some fruit and cold fish left from the night before. They placed Dylan in the middle of a large dugout canoe, stretched out on the bottom where there would be the least movement. In minutes the outboard engine fired up and Dylan felt the boat being shoved out from shore.

Riding down the river was much easier than being carried on a stretcher. Occasionally they plowed across the wake of another boat, but mostly it was calm

"It's a race against time," Uncle Todd shouted to Dylan above the engine's steady drone. "We hired the fastest boat and paid him extra to keep her at full speed. We won't find out until we arrive in Ambunti if they were able to arrange a plane direct to Port Moresby. Pray they can!"

Dylan clenched his teeth against the constant pain and wondered if the ride would ever end. Every half hour, Uncle Todd leaned over and gave him water. After a time, Dylan lost the ability to focus on what was happening around him. Now he endured each second, holding on to his sanity as if clinging to the edge of a cliff. How much longer could he hold on? What would happen if he couldn't? What choice did he have?

When Dylan was certain the trip would never end, the boat slowed and motored ashore in Ambunti. Already, Allen Jackson was calling to somebody on the riverbank to check on the airplane. Dylan heard other voices, then Allen shouted, "Great. We'll have him there in fifteen minutes."

Again, the movement made Dylan grimace with pain, and once more, he threw up, this time mostly fluids. Uncle Todd stretched a mat out on the floor of a small van but it didn't soften the jarring as they bounced down the rough road, headed for the airport beside the river. All Dylan could do was pinch his eyes closed and moan. He knew everyone was trying to help him, but it was killing him. Why couldn't they just leave him alone to die? At least then the pain would end.

Gene spoke loudly to Dylan as they rushed toward the airport. "I'll get on the phone and see if I can arrange some pain meds in Port Moresby while you wait for the flight to Sydney."

Dylan answered with another grimace.

The ride was short. Soon, Dylan felt hands all over him, pulling and shoving and lifting to move him somewhere else. "This is going to be a bit uncomfortable," Allen Jackson said, helping to lift Dylan into a small Cessna aircraft. "There won't be room to lie down. You might be able to stretch your leg out some. See you in Sydney."

When the small plane took off, there was only room for the pilot, Uncle Todd, and Dylan. "We might make it over the top of the peaks today if this weather decides to hold," the Aussie pilot shouted at them as he banked the plane to the southwest.

Dylan opened his eyes to look out, but then bent forward, hugging his leg to drive away the pain and keep from throwing up.

"If you upchuck, you best be doing it into this bag," the pilot informed Dylan, handing him a barf bag.

Dylan wished he had been handed a body bag instead.

# CHAPTER 18

Dylan remembered only portions of the next eight hours: bad turbulence flying over the Owen Stanley Mountains on the way to Port Moresby, clenching his teeth so hard his gums hurt, someone giving him a shot to ease the pain. There was another endless chartered flight to Sydney, followed by an ambulance ride with sirens and flashing lights. Dylan was carried into a hospital, where several nurses and a doctor examined him, then gave him another shot.

Then nothing again.

The next thing Dylan remembered, he woke up feeling drugged and fuzzy in a sunny, air-conditioned hospital room. All he had known for days was heat, mosquitoes, jungle, and pain. Now a television on the wall was broadcasting world news from CNN. He rested in a big, white, padded bed. All his pain had disappeared, and beside the bed sat Uncle Todd, looking tired and unshaven, with a grim stare.

"What happened?" Dylan asked.

"They operated last night," Uncle Todd said hoarsely.

Dylan looked down at his legs but couldn't tell if his leg was missing because of the bunched-up covers.

"What happened?" Dylan asked.

"They saved your life," Uncle Todd said, not offering to explain.

Dylan didn't like the tone of his uncle's voice. He looked down again and tried to wiggle his right foot but still couldn't feel movement. "Did they have to take my leg off?" he asked.

Uncle Todd hesitated. "They said you were very lucky. If it had been one day later, they would have amputated. The way it was, they had to remove a lot of dead tissue. You'll have a few scars and some recovery."

Dylan looked down and found the folded American flag from *Second Ace* still lying by his side. "Thanks for bringing that along," Dylan said.

"Don't thank me," Uncle Todd said. "You had a death grip on that thing until they put you under for surgery. What's so important about that flag?"

Dylan reached down and ran his fingers over the colored cloth, then shrugged. "Not sure — maybe because it was Grandpa's. I never even met him except at family reunions when I was really small. He was just this weird old man. I never dreamed of all the stuff he went through."

"That's the way all old people are," Uncle Todd said. "Someday, you'll be old and some young punk will look at you and think you're just an old fossil and it's darn sure going to burn your butt eight ways from Sunday. But you know what?"

Dylan hesitated, then mumbled weakly, "What?"

"You're going to be so old you won't be able to do anything about it except whiz in your pants because the nurse didn't get to you in time." Uncle Todd shrugged. "There's really only one thing you can do about the whole thing now."

"What's that?" Dylan asked.

"Treat old people with respect. Pay it forward. Then maybe, just maybe, someday when you're too old to hold back a fart, some young kid will respect you for who you are."

Big tears flooded Dylan's eyes. "I'm just a screw-up," he said, his voice close to breaking.

Uncle Todd smirked. "If life ended today, I'd probably agree with you. But it hasn't ended yet. For you, life is just beginning. Maybe this trip will screw your head on straight."

"It's too late. I'll be in eighth grade next year. You were probably at the top of your class and an Eagle Scout by my age."

Uncle Todd allowed a thin smile. "See, there you go again, feeling sorry for yourself and judging people without know-ing the truth." He pointed at the wrinkles on his own neck. "These aren't wrinkles from growing old," he said. "These are stretch marks left from getting my own head screwed on straight. By the time I graduated from high school, I had a rap sheet twice as long as yours. Your grandfather had the judge give me a choice — either go to jail or join the military. That's when I joined the Marines."

"You didn't join 'cause you were patriotic?" Dylan asked.

Uncle Todd laughed. "I couldn't have cared less about this country. Everything was a joke, until Vietnam. I still have questions about that war, but I will tell you this: When you see death, you grow up real quick and start to think. When I came back from Vietnam, I felt like the whole country was in a fishbowl and I was the only one on the outside. No matter what I had done, no matter how many lives I had saved, no matter how brave I was or how many medals I'd earned, the country ignored me. They ignored me and all the other soldiers who fought."

Dylan twisted at a corner of the bedsheet. "Does Mom know what happened to me?"

"She had to give her permission for the operation. She's plenty worried, but knows there wasn't an amputation. She was . . ." Uncle Todd's face took on a pained expression. "She said she was going to fly out here immediately. I had to practically order her not to. You'll be here in the hospital a few more days, and then it's time to go home. When you're up to it, you need to call her."

"What can I tell her? That I screwed up again?"

"Tell her whatever you want. I do know this — she's never given up on you. You're the one I'm worried about. You've already given up on yourself."

———

Three times a day, nurses changed the dressing on Dylan's ankle. Twice a day, he took antibiotics, and this time he didn't spit out the medications. By the second night, he quit having hot and cold flashes. Slowly his insect bites faded. What the hospital couldn't treat were his troubled thoughts. Dylan hated closing his eyes, fearing he would wake up back in the jungle.

Gene, Allen, and Quentin stopped in when they arrived back in Sydney. They had little to say as they surrounded the hospital bed. Dylan felt like he had let everyone down. The whole month's trip had been changed now because of him. "I'm sorry for everything," he kept saying.

"Hey, you found *Second Ace*," Quentin reminded him again.

"You get well and let us know how you're doing," Allen Jackson said after being there only a few minutes.

"I'll call all of you," Dylan promised.

And then they left. The three planned on touring Australia for several weeks and returning to the US on their scheduled flight. By then, Dylan would be back in Wisconsin with his mother. Uncle Todd would be back in Oregon, no longer having to deal with his pain-in-the-butt nephew.

"Did you call your mom yet?" Uncle Todd asked each morning and evening when he visited the hospital.

"I'll call her soon," Dylan kept promising, still not knowing what to say.

Finally he summoned the courage. He made the call one evening with Uncle Todd sitting nearby and staring at him intently.

"Hello?" the distant voice answered.

"Hello, Mom, this is Dylan."

"How are you?" she asked, her voice guarded.

Dylan found it hard to talk. "I'm good," he said. "I can't wait to get home."

"The hospital says you'll be out in a couple of days, and then Todd said he's buying you a ticket home on Wednesday."

"I kind of screwed things up over here," Dylan said meekly.

There was deafening silence on the phone.

"I'm done being stupid," Dylan said.

"You always say that," she said.

"This time I mean it. I can't wait to tell you everything that happened."

"I'm sure you'll have quite a story," she said.

Dylan could tell from her voice that she still didn't believe him. What could he possibly do to convince her that he had changed?

"Mom," he said. "I know that Dad leaving wasn't because he didn't love us."

"He never quit loving us," she said. "But you've never believed that. Now I feel as if I've lost you both."

"You haven't lost me," Dylan said. "Not anymore."

She hesitated. "Listen, we'll talk when you get back." She spoke as if she wanted to end the phone call.

"Okay," Dylan said. "I'll see you." Suddenly, tears flooded his eyes. He took a deep breath. "And, Mom . . . I love y —"

Dylan heard a dial tone. Already she had hung up.

He slowly hung up as Uncle Todd eyed him closely.

"Mom said you're getting me a ticket home on Wednesday," Dylan choked.

Uncle Todd nodded.

"What are you going to do when we get back?" Dylan asked.

"I think I'll head back to Gresham the same day. I've got things to get done. I'll fly as far as Los Angeles with you."

"I know it costs extra, but can I go back to Oregon with you before going home? I'll earn the money and pay you back."

"Why?"

"I want to see Frank Bower again."

"What for?"

"I want to give him this flag." Dylan held up the American flag that he still kept by his side on the bed.

"I'll give that to him for you," Uncle Todd said.

Dylan shook his head. "No, I have to give it to him myself. It won't be the same otherwise."

Uncle Todd studied Dylan before answering. "Why you?"

"I'm done being stupid," Dylan insisted.

Uncle Todd turned in his chair to face Dylan. "You know, I almost thought you were sorry before, too. When you first met Frank and he told you his story, for half a second I thought you had learned something. But then you were right back to complaining, feeling sorry for yourself, and thinking you were the center of the universe."

Dylan blinked back his tears. "I think Mom still thinks the same thing. So what do I do? How can I change if you guys don't give me the chance?"

"You've had a hundred chances. Maybe you should start by being honest. Not just with other people, but with yourself."

"And how will you ever know if I have?" Dylan blurted.

Uncle Todd leaned back in his chair and gave Dylan a long, hard stare.

Dylan met his stare, but not with attitude. He just wanted Uncle Todd to know he was a man and didn't have to look down.

Suddenly Uncle Todd slapped the arm of the chair and stood. "Okay, I'll bite one more time. I'll make the ticket so you fly into Portland overnight before going home. Please don't make me sorry I trusted you."

———

Using crutches, Dylan left the hospital to spend their last night in Sydney at the hotel with Uncle Todd. Hobbling everywhere they went, Dylan looked around town a little, then they went out later for a big cheeseburger, fries, and a chocolate shake. Every bite made Dylan remember the grasshoppers he had eaten just to stay alive. Never in his life had a cheeseburger tasted so good. Uncle Todd let him order seconds. He ate until he was absolutely stuffed.

"What are you going to do with the rest of your summer?" Uncle Todd asked.

Dylan answered without hesitation. "I'm going to do whatever I can to help Mom out. She doesn't earn a lot, and I know she usually spends any extra money on me instead of herself." Dylan paused and added, "And I will pay you back the extra flight cost of stopping in Oregon."

Uncle Todd laughed. "Well, you're not even in eighth grade, so don't expect to be pulling in the big bucks mowing lawns. Don't worry, I'll take care of the extra airfare. Helping your mom sounds real good, but words are cheap. Let's see if it actually happens."

"It's as good as done," Dylan promised.

———

Dylan packed his backpack early the next morning. He was still taking his antibiotics and malaria medication, and would need to for some time. By mid-morning they had cleared customs and were in the air flying home. They flew on a Boeing 747, and the plane was huge. Dylan tried several times to start conversations, but Uncle Todd kept to himself, answering Dylan's questions with only "Yup" or "Nope."

No matter what Uncle Todd had said about one more chance, it was obvious he had already written Dylan off as a loser. "Will you go back to see *Second Ace* sometime?" Dylan asked, trying one more time to break the ice.

Uncle Todd just shrugged and said, "Who knows."

Dylan turned and stared out the window. "Who knows" was as bad as "whatever."

For Dylan, this trip to Papua New Guinea was like something out of a science fiction story. Less than two weeks ago, he had been flying from the United States, angry at the world, and never having met Allen, Gene, or Quentin. He hadn't cared about a B-17 bomber called *Second Ace*, and he had resented being with his uncle.

Now it felt as if he had been through some kind of time warp. All of his experiences in the jungles of PNG already seemed like a dream or an experience from another lifetime. Had it all been real? What puzzled Dylan most was when he looked in the mirror. Who was that baby-faced punk kid he was looking at? Was he just looking at someone who would go back to being angry and doing stupid things, blaming everything on everybody else?

Even Dylan didn't know that answer for sure.

# CHAPTER 19

During the flight, Dylan's ankle ached. He swallowed the pills the doctor had given him to curb the pain, but they made him sleepy. He slept most of the way across the Pacific. When they landed in Los Angeles, he felt like a zombie. They had a two-hour layover before flying on to Portland. Still Uncle Todd gave Dylan the silent treatment, as if he were a criminal. Maybe going to Oregon before returning home was a mistake.

By the time they arrived in Portland, they had been flying most of the last twenty-four hours. Uncle Todd opened the front door to his condo in Gresham. It was almost dark. "When do you want to stop by the nursing home to see Frank Bower?" Uncle Todd asked. "Tonight? Or tomorrow before I take you to the airport?"

Dylan yawned hard. "After we get some sleep."

"Whatever you want," Uncle Todd said. "That's what you usually do."

Dylan knew his Uncle Todd had every reason in the world for not trusting him, but he wanted to explain that he had changed, and not just a little. He really did feel differently now about the world, and himself. But starting a conversation now would be like trying to light a match to look inside a powder keg. "How about tomorrow morning?" Dylan suggested.

"I said whatever you want," Uncle Todd repeated, heading for his room. "As long as it's early enough to get you to the airport."

Still carrying his backpack and using his crutches, Dylan hobbled up the stairs to his room. As much as he had hated Uncle Todd's constant lectures before they left, now it bugged him even worse to get the silent treatment.

Dylan lay on the bed with clean sheets and no mosquitoes, listening to the many noises from the street. A car drove past with a radio blasting. Dylan didn't like loud sounds anymore, but he understood them. Each sound he heard tonight he could place in his brain neatly and explain it. But then he remembered the jungle, lying under the damp moss, mosquitoes so thick he choked on them, suffering through sweats and chills, and hearing strange growls and screeches in the underbrush. Alone.

Dylan felt as if he had a stranger's brain in his head. Who was it that was really lying here awake in the guest room of Uncle Todd's small yellow condo? Before leaving the US, Dylan had needed to be in control. The angrier he became, the more he blamed others. The bigger the chip on his shoulder, the more attitude he projected. The more other people tried to help him, the more he laughed in their faces. But in the jungle, that control had disappeared. The more attitude he displayed, the more the world slammed him and tried to kill him.

So now who was Dylan Barstow? What did he want to do? How would he act tomorrow morning when the sun came up? There had been something safe about carrying an attitude around. Dylan had loved the disgusted looks from adults when he wore his pants low. He felt in control when he thumbed his nose in someone's face. Whenever he dismissed someone's thoughts with a "whatever," it did mean he didn't care how people felt or what people did. If he was always angry, he didn't have to look in the mirror and take responsibility. He had always been the center of the universe. Dylan Barstow's universe.

But now he felt like a fish that had been dumped from its fishbowl. Suddenly Dylan had discovered a world that wasn't so simple — so small. No longer did things look so wonderful back inside the little protected world he had created for himself in Wisconsin. Dylan wondered what would happen if he quit thinking only of himself? What if he quit blaming his father for dying? What if he were to be respectful? Take the risk of being hurt again? Give up his attitude? Give up control? Then what?

It would be like a fighter exposing his bare chest. People could make fun of him because he cared. People could hurt him. Friends might tease him. Not that he had any real friends — just other kids protecting themselves.

Dylan clenched his fists under the covers. Dad had shown him many pictures of villagers crowding around the trucks where aid workers were handing out food. To Dylan, the people had seemed like animals, climbing over each other's backs, shoving and pushing, fighting for little scraps of anything. He had blamed them and everybody else in the whole world for taking his father away. Dad's death had hurt so very much.

But now Dylan remembered crawling through grass in the swamps on his hands and knees, stuffing grasshoppers in his mouth and squeezing muddy water out of his shirt to drink. It was no different, except in the swamps there had been nobody to even offer help. Dylan also knew that the people who crowded the trucks in Darfur were victims. They had been born in Sudan. They didn't deserve the cruel genocide that was killing them. They hadn't done anything to cause their starvation. It hadn't been their fault!

That's what made Dylan ashamed now. He hadn't caused Dad's death. But neither had everybody else he blamed. It had been an accident. Still he had blamed Dad for dying. He had used that as an excuse for breaking into the junkyard and skipping school. He had picked fights at school and stolen things. He was the one who spit out the malaria pills and walked away from the safety of their group in the jungle. Everything had been his fault. He could blame others, but that would be lying to himself.

One feeling overwhelmed Dylan. It was the same feeling

he had felt lying half dead under the screw tree covered with moss in the middle of the jungle. Overwhelming loneliness. Nobody knew his feelings. And nobody probably cared anymore. Dylan's eyes watered. He wanted to run downstairs and wake Uncle Todd up and say, "Hey, look at all the things I'm thinking. I'm not stupid. I'm really sorry. I don't always have to protect myself with attitude. Please, give me just one more chance."

But even as he swung his feet to the floor, he heard his uncle's muffled snoring downstairs. Dylan crawled back under the covers.

---

A heavy drizzle fell as Dylan woke and heard his uncle moving around downstairs. It took a couple of seconds to remember where he was. He would never have admitted it, but he missed his uncle's "Wakee wakee wakee!"

Dylan sat up and slowly unwrapped the gauze from his ankle. The doctor had said if there wasn't any infection or drainage, it would be okay to remove the bandages after getting home. He said it would be better for the skin to get air.

Dylan dressed and used only one of his crutches to get down the stairs. His ankle felt much better. "Good morning," he said, trying to sound cheery as he entered the kitchen.

"Good morning," Uncle Todd said, picking up a newspaper to start reading. "There's food in the refrigerator if you want breakfast." His voice was matter-of-fact.

"Do you want some, too?" Dylan asked.

"I've already eaten," Uncle Todd said and kept reading.

Dylan fried himself a couple of eggs, not because he was hungry, but because he wanted to prove to Uncle Todd that he wasn't this spoiled punk kid who couldn't do anything for himself. But it didn't make any difference. Uncle Todd never said a single word or looked up once from his newspaper.

When Dylan finished eating, he hurried upstairs to get his luggage and to get the flag, then came back down and asked, "Can we go see Frank Bower now on the way to the airport?"

"You might want to call him first," Uncle Todd commented.

"I want to surprise him."

"*Whatever* you want," Uncle Todd said.

Dylan *wanted* to scream. It was as if Uncle Todd had totally written him off. "You don't even care if I give this flag to Frank Bower, do you?" Dylan said, his voice accusing.

Uncle Todd turned to face Dylan. "I care. I just don't like doing anything on this planet that wastes my time," he said. "Babysitting a spoiled kid who can't take a crap without thinking the world owes him toilet paper is wasting my time."

—

The drizzle had turned to rain as they drove to the Garden Acres Rest Home. It wasn't much fun riding in the '62 Corvette with Uncle Todd in a bad mood, not speaking.

"You want me to wait in the car?" Uncle Todd asked, pulling to a stop outside the sprawling brick rest home.

"Can you come in with me?" Dylan asked.

"Whatever you want," Uncle Todd said, crawling out.

Dylan stood in the rain, holding the American flag from *Second Ace*. He looked across the top of the Corvette at his uncle. "Why don't you just say 'whatever'?!" he shouted. "That's what you mean. Now you're the one saying 'screw you'! You're the one telling me my words don't count! You're the one not showing me respect."

"Maybe because I'm still not sure you deserve respect!" Uncle Todd shot back.

"You'll never know!" yelled Dylan. "Not if you don't give me another chance." When Uncle Todd didn't answer, Dylan shouted again, "Is that it, then? I'm a screw-up, so good-bye and don't ever come back? Adios!"

Uncle Todd looked back at Dylan. Ignoring the rain that had become a downpour, he pointed his finger at Dylan and shouted, "Do you know what it would have been like to call my brother's widow and say, 'I'm sorry, but I got your son killed!'? I never slept one minute until we found you. You were my responsibility, and I failed! I won't be making that mistake again. Go kill yourself on your own time!"

Thunder rumbled across the sky.

Dylan glared back at his uncle and saw a deep hurt in his eyes. He realized how much Uncle Todd must have cared. But now it was too late. Fighting back his tears, Dylan turned and limped without crutches across the parking lot through the deluge of rain. He tried to protect the flag under his arm.

Uncle Todd followed.

"You sure picked a rainy day to visit," said the receptionist as they entered the front door, drenched.

"Can you tell me where to find Frank Bower?" Dylan asked.

The receptionist pointed down the hall. "Go ask at the nurses' station. I'm new and can't keep the patients straight."

With Uncle Todd following, Dylan limped down the hallway, stepping around several old people with walkers or in wheelchairs. He recognized the red-haired nurse at the nurse's station. "We came to see Frank Bower again," Dylan announced. "Can you tell me where he's at?"

The nurse recognized them, too, and hesitated. "Are you family?"

"No, I just wanted to give him this." Dylan held up the flag.

The nurse looked at Dylan and at the flag. "I probably shouldn't be telling you this if you're not family, but Frank died last Thursday. He had a heart attack. Died in his sleep."

Dylan stood, stunned. "Died?" he said. "I just talked with him two weeks ago."

The nurse nodded. "He was quite a guy."

Dylan spoke, almost frantically. "Did you know he was a waist gunner during the war? He flew twenty-five missions and belonged to the Lucky Bast —"

"I'm sorry to interrupt you," said the nurse, coming from behind the counter. "But we're two aides short this morning so I'm alone on the floor. Is there anything else I can help you with?" She started down the hallway, not waiting for an answer.

Dylan shook his head as he watched her disappear. "No," he whispered. "You can't help me. Nobody can anymore."

# CHAPTER 20

Dylan hung his head for a moment. Frank Bower being dead was the last straw. Somehow holding on to the American flag and bringing it back to the US for Frank had been a mission of sorts. Dylan knew he had screwed up everything else, but that was the one single thing he had planned on doing that was right. And now he couldn't even do that.

"Are you satisfied now?" Uncle Todd asked.

Dylan grew suddenly angry. "No, I'm not satisfied," he shot back. "This isn't about me being satisfied. You can be mad at me, and you have every reason to be. But now you're being a jerk. I thought that was my job."

For a moment, Uncle Todd looked like he was going to blow up. His face twitched and a vein stood out on his neck. But then he motioned and started toward the front door. "Let's get out of here."

Dylan was turning to follow when he heard a loud grunt from a side hallway. "Help, please help!" cried a weak voice.

Without thinking, Dylan ran down the hall. Again the desperate voice sounded. Dylan discovered an old man with silver hair lying on the floor inside his room beside the toilet, his pants still down. His wheelchair lay beside him. It looked like he'd been trying to go to the bathroom and had fallen while swinging himself onto the toilet. He grimaced.

Dylan ran to his side. "Are you okay?" he asked.

"No, dang it, I'm not okay. My wheelchair got away from me. I have my pants down and I'm lying on the floor. A person ain't okay when they're like that."

Dylan set the folded flag on the dresser and grabbed the man under his arms. His frail body felt like a skeleton as Dylan lifted him onto the toilet.

"I'm already done crapping," the man scolded. "I need to get back in my wheelchair."

Obediently, Dylan set the wheelchair upright. Once more he lifted the old man and swung him into his chair. With each move, it felt like the old man's bones would break. "Are you okay now?" Dylan asked.

"You're never okay when you're my age," the man said. "But I'm as good as it gets."

"Need anything else?" Dylan asked.

"Yeah, a young body like yours and a cuter nurse."

Dylan smiled. "Well, I gotta go." He was turning to leave when he spotted a small medal pin on the headrest of the old man's wheelchair. It was a VFW pin. "Were you in the military?" Dylan asked.

"Guess I was," the old man said. "Ever heard of the Bataan Death March?"

Dylan shook his head.

The old man pointed a finger at Dylan. "I have some family coming to see me this morning, but come back this afternoon and I'll tell you what I went through. Compared to the Death March, going to hell would have been a vacation."

"I have to go to the airport," Dylan explained. He looked at the man in his wheelchair and then picked up the folded flag off the dresser. "But can I give you this?"

The old man reached out his bony hand. His fingers trembled as he ran them across the red, white and blue cloth. A pained expression crossed his face. "A lot of soldiers went through hell to protect that old flag."

"Can I give it to you?" Dylan asked again. "I found it in a B-17 bomber in Papua New Guinea. My grandfather had it."

The old man pulled his hand back from the flag, then shook his head sadly. "No," he said. "That flag don't need to be in no skunk-hole place like this sitting on some old fossil's dresser. You find a better place."

"You're not an old fossil," Dylan blurted. He had come to hate that word.

"If you say so," the old man said.

"I say so," Dylan said. "What's your name?"

"John Taylor. And what's yours?"

"Dylan Barstow."

The old man nodded and extended his hand. "Glad to meet you, Dylan Barstow. You sure are a fine young man. I'll bet your parents are proud of you."

Dylan shook the old man's hand but ignored the comment. "I'm glad to meet you, too, John Taylor. I might not know anything about this Death March, but I do know one thing I learned getting that flag."

"What was that, son?"

"Freedom is never free."

John Taylor trembled as he spoke. "No, it sure ain't, son. It's never free."

Dylan turned and discovered Uncle Todd standing in the doorway watching all that had gone on. "Maybe you should come back this afternoon and hear about the Bataan Death March," Uncle Todd said.

"I have to catch the plane," Dylan said.

Uncle Todd shrugged. "Your mom might understand if you wanted to stay one more day, but that's up to you," he said. "You think about it."

"But I thought you were mad at me."

"I am. But maybe this is more important."

Dylan allowed a smile. "I would love to hear about the Death March," he told John Taylor. "I'll call Mom and tell her why I'm staying one more day. I do need to get home — I'm missing her."

"Ready to go?" Uncle Todd asked, his voice softer.

Dylan nodded. "I guess."

Without speaking, they ran through the pouring rain to the parking lot, rushing to crawl into the Corvette. Dylan gripped the folded flag and looked out the side window in silence. Big raindrops ran down the glass like tears. Dylan blinked, but the raindrops continued.

Again, neither of them spoke as Uncle Todd drove from the parking lot. They were halfway home when suddenly Uncle Todd pulled the Corvette over to the side of the road.

"Is something wrong?" Dylan asked.

The rain had let up, but a light drizzle still misted the air as Uncle Todd eyed Dylan. "That's what I'm trying to decide." He continued staring. Finally a soft smile melted his intense expression. He looked out at the gray, drizzly sky. "It's a great day for drifting a Corvette. Do you think you can do it at fifty miles per hour?"

"But you think I'm a screw-up."

Uncle Todd shook his head. "I would never let a screw-up even touch my Corvette!"

THE END

# EPILOGUE

Five months after the discovery of the B-17 bomber *Second Ace*, a Marine task force completed its investigation and recovery of remains from the wreckage. Because many remains could not be identified, an official full-dress ceremony was held at the Tomb of the Unknown Soldier in Arlington National Cemetery. As the individual who officially discovered the wreckage, Dylan Barstow was invited to present a wreath at the tomb.

On a blustery winter's day, an honor guard gave a twenty-one-gun salute. The ceremony was witnessed by relatives of the lost crew. Also among the small group stood one very proud mother, as well as the other members of the search team, Gene and Quentin Cooper, Todd Barstow, and Allen Jackson. They all watched as Dylan Barstow walked solemnly to an easel placed in front of the tomb. There he hung a green spruce wreath woven with nine roses — the number of crew members who perished on a stormy day back in 1943 in a swamp in Papua New Guinea.

When the wreath had been hung, Dylan reached inside his jacket and removed a folded American flag. He paused for a moment to touch the cloth one last time and to remember how the flag had come into his possession. Then he rested the flag gently on the wreath. "Thanks, Grandpa," he whispered. "Thanks, Dad," he added. He paused one more time. "And thanks, Kanzi, whoever you are."

Before leaving the grave, Dylan knelt and placed a simple note on the marble tomb. The note was written in the messy handwriting of a young teenager. It said simply,

## Freedom is never free!

For the record, not that it mattered anymore, but Dylan Barstow's pants hung down a little bit that day only because it was more comfortable.

# AUTHOR'S NOTE

I must say that during the writing of each of my novels, it is not me who creates and changes the story as much as it is the story that changes me. I was well aware of many of the historical facts of the Second World War, but after hearing the personal accounts of bravery during my research for *Jungle of Bones*, I was humbled to tears. The adage that "freedom is never free" became more than simple words. Those words became very real and not only imprinted themselves on my mind but are now chiseled like stone in my heart.

Ben Mikaelsen

# ABOUT THE AUTHOR

Ben Mikaelsen is the winner of the International Reading Association Award and the Western Writer's Golden Spur Award. His novels have been nominated for and have won many state Readers' Choice awards. These novels include *Rescue Josh McGuire, Sparrow Hawk Red, Stranded, Countdown, Petey, Touching Spirit Bear, Red Midnight, Tree Girl,* and *Ghost of Spirit Bear.* Ben is known for his in-depth research and the magical worlds he creates. This research has taken him around the world from the North Pole to Africa. He has made over 1,000 parachute jumps, boated the length of the Mississippi, cycled in nearly every state, lived with the homeless in Mexico, raced sled dogs, and ridden a horse from Minnesota to Oregon. Ben lives in a log cabin near Bozeman, Montana, with his wife, Connie. For twenty-six years he raised a 750-pound black bear, Buffy, that he saved from a research facility. Visit Ben online at www.benmikaelsen.com.